Contents

PREFACE

I have quoted Remarque's *Im Westen nichts Neues* from the edition I prepared originally for Methuen's *Twentieth Century Texts* in 1984, and page references are to the corrected reprint (London: Routledge, 1988). I have been concerned to avoid repeating material from the introduction and notes, although I have sometimes developed more fully here points adumbrated briefly in that edition or in my subsequent talk on the work for the series *Exeter Tapes*. The variations in Remarque's text revisions are not significant for the present study. I have here concentrated in particular upon the one-character perspective and the different possibilities in the war-novel; on the realities of the First World War and the philosophical questioning of the war itself; and upon the theme of the lost generation and the relationship between the the novel and its sequel, *Der Weg zurück*. In terms of reception, I have tried to keep in mind three basic questions: what view are we given of the First World War itself? What were the implications when the novel appeared during the Weimar Republic? And - most important of all - what does it have to say to a modern audience? The emphasis is upon the work as a novel, and the historical backgrounds to the First World War or to the Weimar Republic (easily accessible from other sources) are accordingly less fully treated.

I have attempted, too, to place the work into a literary context, and have listed in the bibliography beside a selection from the (increasing) body of scholarly studies of Remarque, a number of other war-novels of various kinds (several of which are mentioned in my text) which may usefully be compared with *Im Westen nichts Neues*. Many of these have been reprinted, but some have not, though they can sometimes be found in libraries or second-hand bookshops. The list is not intended to be devoured wholesale, but is for sampling.

I am indebted for many points to those students at Stirling with whom I have discussed the work in detail in Honours seminars on the Weimar war novel, and also, as so often before, to my wife for comments on the manuscript, and to my friend and colleague Mark Ward for scholarly and technical assistance.

Brian Murdoch
Stirling, January 1991

PREFACE TO SECOND EDITION

For this new edition some new bibliographical material (including my own translation of the novel, published by Cape in 1994) has been added, and some minor changes and corrections have been made to the text. I should like to express my gratitude to Gill Hughes and the Library of the Taylor Institution in Oxford, for assistance during a recent visiting fellowship, and especially to Dr Thomas Schneider of the Erich-Maria-Remarque-Archiv in Osnabrück for his most helpful comments.

Brian Murdoch
Magdalen College, Oxford/Stirling University, December 1994

Chapter One

Endlich Klarheit über Remarque und sein Buch
Im Westen nichts Neues

The Background to the Novel

Erich Paul Remark was born in Osnabrück in 1898, and he changed his name to the form in which it was to become famous, Erich Maria Remarque, largely to dissociate himself from an early book which he had published under his original name. He was certainly never called Kramer, although that particular myth dies hard. His date of birth is significant in view of his best-known novel, however: he reached the age of eighteen in the middle of the First World War, served in the German forces and was wounded, spending time in a military hospital. His experiences in the First World War led him - after a less than succesful period as schoolteacher and writer - to produce in 1928 his novel *Im Westen nichts Neues*, which was to provide for him the rare distinction of being a German writer of a world bestseller, of what must remain, in fact, the best-known novel of the First World War, with a title that is proverbial in German and English alike. The details of the genesis of the novel are well-known and need little rehearsing here.[1] Remarque's work was accepted (after some initial setbacks) by the massive Berlin publisher, Ullstein, and produced in a slightly expurgated form as a serial in their journal *Vossische Zeitung*, then later in full as a novel which had - for a variety of reasons - an instant and unprecedented commercial success. Some of this was due to its timing: the war had been over for ten years, time for its horrors to be digested and transmuted into literary form, but the Weimar Republic, of which it was still a product, was already experiencing problems on which the novel and more particularly its sequel, *Der Weg zurück* have some bearing.

The novel was, however, not something entirely new. There had already been major successes for writings about the First World War, whether they saw it as an adventure or whether they condemned it. Already at the end of the war the French novelist Henri Barbusse had produced a powerful and much-read work called *Le Feu*, published in German as *Das Feuer*, which condemned the war it presented from the

---

[1] See in particular Hubert Rüter, *Remarque: Im Westen nichts Neues*, (Paderborn, 1980), esp. pp. 58-64 for details of the various forms in which the text appeared. Quotation here is from my own edition of the full text (revised edition, 1988; I hope I may be permitted here to correct the residual but unfortunate misprint of "Flachskopf" as "Flaschkopf" on p. 83!).

point of view of the ordinary soldier. On the other hand, the memoirs of a German pilot called von Plüschow, with the significant title *Die Abenteuer des Fliegers von Tsingtau*, originally published well before Remarque, was republished and sold well for the same publisher, Ullstein, a firm which also published a number of other war novels. An anti-war novel, Arnold Zweig's *Der Streit um den Sergeanten Grischa* was a best-seller in German in 1927 and was equally popular in English in 1928. It is far more complex than Remarque's work, however, and uses a single incident within the war to show the effects of the German military machine, rather than illustrating much of the war directly.

Part of Remarque's success was due to Ullstein and their advertising efforts. The work was given very considerable publicity, and modern marketing played a considerable role in the promotion of the original text and, indeed, of the translation. But publicity alone did not, of course, sell the book. Its main points were not that it was an anti-war novel as such, but the way in which it presented the war, the style and the content. The style is simple and effective, and easy to assimilate: it moves rapidly between passages of vivid and varied descriptions of events and passages of personal feelings about the war, all placed in the mouth of the first-person narrator of most of the novel, the young soldier Paul Bäumer, with whom the reader can identify readily. The rapid alternation of incidents, and of these passages with more thoughtful ones keep the interest-level high. The plot as such is relatively simple, too, and the fact that the novel distills much of the experience of the First World War into a relatively small space will have contributed to its popularity, the more so as it neither presents nor demands any historical overview. Indeed, only a few weeks of 1917 are shown in any detail, with the last year of the war condensed into two short and rather different final chapters. To look at whole strategies would be impossible. Remarque shows us instead the effects of the war on a very small group of people, and what is more, on a group that can be seen as typical of many, if not most of those who fought.

Reading novels of the First World War presents the modern reader with a variety of critical problems, and several questions are raised by such novels, for which *Im Westen nichts Neues* has come to be a kind of yardstick. First, the term 'novel' is placed into question from the start; the theme is clearly a genuine historical one, and the historical details of the Great War itself provide an extrinsic structuring visible most clearly, perhaps, in the fictive diaries of the war. A neglected novel by a woman writer, Adrienne Thomas' *Die Katrin wird Soldat* is in diary form, so that although the diarist is unaware of the significance of approaching dates, the reader awaits August 4, 1914, for example, and knows, when a character comments that the war will be over soon, that this is not true. In Remarque, too, the war becomes increasingly hopeless over the period covered - roughly from 1917 to the end of 1918 - and the reader is aware of the significance of Bäumer's death at a time when the sailors were already mutinying in Kiel and Wilhelmshaven, and the war was all but finished. The danger, of course, is that the shift from novel to historical novel to historical document is all too easy. Remarque's work contains at least one historical character - Kaiser Wilhelm II - and many of the incidents are based on the author's own experience. Yet the work is still a novel, and it is - or can be - dangerous to take this work written in 1928 as an eye-witness account of events of 1917 with the force of an historical document. We have to question even writers like Theodor Plievier, whose novel of the navy, *Des Kaisers Kulis*, was written as a kind of counterpart to Remarque's work, when he suddenly tells us

> Hier ist kein Roman. Hier ist ein Dokument.
> Und dann: ich bin doch auch dabei gewesen.[2]

Many critics have taken Remarque as a source for the history of the war, and amongst those who reacted to the work with some violence was the Kropp whose book gave the title to this chapter. He had been in hospital with Remarque (who used his name - but that seemingly is all) and denounces Remarque as a liar for describing events which he, Kropp, did not see and probably did not happen in the hospital at that time. He above all - and those who demanded implicitly that Remarque be equated with Bäumer, even though Bäumer is ultimately killed - falls into the trap of taking a novel for something which it is not. It has to be borne in mind that *Im Westen nichts Neues* is a novel set in what even at the time of writing was an historical period, and not a history source-book, though its content may well interpret historical events.

The work was written in 1928, not in 1918, and the point has fairly been made that it looks to its historical present as well as to the past. It is not just a novel of the First World War, but of the Weimar Republic, the government in Germany set up in some turmoil after the war, which eventually collapsed with Hitler's gaining of power and establishment of a Third Reich in 1933. This novel and other war novels of the period need to be considered on three quite separate levels. The first is historical: what picture is presented of the First World War, a quite

[2] Theodor Plievier, *Des Kaisers Kulis* (1929), (Munich, 1984), p. 240. Here as with other novels quoted I have used the most readily available current edition, usually the paperback.

specific historical event, details of which can be found in history books based on reports, memories, documents, even films of the war itself? How real is the picture, and how complete? - we might also say, how fair? - although we must avoid the danger of glib acceptance of the work as an eye-witness document. The second level is that of the period of writing: the work was written ten years after the events it shows, and its initial great popularity was in Weimar Germany, a politically already somewhat shaky state, and one in which people of all political colours looked back and tried to come to terms with a war in which many of them had been involved, and for which they sought a meaning. We are more familiar with the concept of "Vergangenheitsbewältigung" in the period after the Second World War, but it was as important in the Weimar peiod. We must in this case be aware of a different danger: that to which terms like "the personal heresy" or "the intentional fallacy" have (somewhat unfairly) been applied, and which concentrates exclusively upon the author's intention and the reception of the work at the time of writing. The meaning of *Im Westen nichts Neues* for the Weimar Republic is indeed of some interest, but concentration upon it leads to a concentration on only some of the themes, and worse, it can easily lead to a failure to see the wood for the trees.[3]

The third level is perhaps the most important for the modern reader: what is the significance of the novel for the present? Knowledge of some increasingly distant events, concerned with a war fought in what is now a primitive fashion is one possible benefit, of course, as indeed is the fact that the novel can also give us an insight into its own age - that of the Weimar Republic. These functions are either historical or elegaic, perhaps. More to the point, however, the novel can for us become not only a novel about the First World War, but a war novel in a more general sense, a novel showing us something about war, and about the results of war on the body and on the mind of ordinary men. It is a novel whose subject is war - to adapt the words of Wilfred Owen - and the pity of war. If in the Weimar Republic its message was ultimately lost - Herbert Read wrote a paper called "The Failure of the War Books" and the anti-war novels did indeed fail to prevent a Second World War - the novel survives because it makes a valid point that war as such is appalling.

Im Westen nichts Neues has a single central figure, the narrator, who is a private soldier in the First World War. The dates are imprecise, although we may deduce that Paul Bäumer, the narrator, volunteered

---

[3] Thus for example R. Littlejohns, "Der Krieg hat uns für alles verdorben: the Real Theme of *Im Westen nichts Neues*", *Modern Languages*, 70 (1989), 89-94. If the novel were actually to have a single 'real theme' it would clearly be that of war itself; but of course it has several themes.

after pressure from a school teacher and joined the army with his entire school class, probably not at the very beginning of the war. The novel begins in chronological terms in 1917, but there are flashbacks to the beginning of Paul Bäumer's career as a soldier. We are not, however, shown the beginning of the war, nor are we shown the end of it, since the narrator is killed in October 1918. The whole picture of the Great War that the novel presents, however, is one of a war which had come to seem endless and wearisome at the beginning of the novel, and which was to become progressively worse as the soldiers upon whom the novel centres are gradually killed and the army in which they are fighting is clearly defeated, even if the culmination, the death of Bäumer himself, occurs just before the end. The novel falls, effectively, into two parts, each consisting of half-a-dozen chapters, these containing in their turn for the most part a variety of incidents. Although the novel is not subtitled - as was Barbusse's, for example - "the story of a squad", the concentration is upon Bäumer and his immediate group, including some of his former classmates, and some others, either younger men who have joined up from working on the land, or who are older, as in the case of Stanislaus Katczinsky, who becomes Bäumer's close friend and mentor. The perspective, therefore, is that of the lowest ranks of the army, and we rarely go any further in the military hierarchy. The men are put through (excessively rigorous) basic training by a corporal, who becomes more of an enemy to Bäumer and his fellows than the opposing armies; a cook-corporal is equally a figure of opposition, but beyond this one can actually enumerate the officers appearing in the work: a couple of lieutenants, or perhaps only one, a martinet major and once the Kaiser himself. The concentration is on the military experiences, then, of a finite group of rankers on the Western Front.

The work moves easily between incidents. At the beginning the men have returned after a spell in the front-line trenches, in which they have suffered heavy losses. From the few historical or geographical references this seems to be during what in English is known as Third Ypres, the Flanders offensive in 1917, and often tagged with the name Passchendael. They look back to their induction into the army, and visit one of their number dying in a field-hospital. This is continued in the second chapter, which also looks back, fills in details of the various characters, and ends with the death of the schoolboy-soldier, and also in the third, which introduces us primarily to Katczinsky. In these chapters, as later, direct action is alternated with discussion and with individual thoughts on the part of the narrator, Bäumer himself, giving us three levels in the structure. The first of these is responded to objectively: we watch things happen and may draw our own conclusions, and the actions are all to do with the war itself. The second level is conditioned by the comments of the participants, although the reader must also make a decision on whether to agree with one of the views expressed, or to take the discussion objectively too. The third level is much more clearly directed: the reader is in the mind of a young man involved with the war, and in this case the thoughts are very much directed in the first instance, the objectivity coming later when the reader steps away from Bäumer himself, or rather: is torn away from Bäumer when he is killed.

The fourth chapter moves back to the front, though not to fighting, but to a state of being under fire, and the fifth offers another respite, with additional reflection and flashback, although the corporal whose excesses during the training period were discussed earlier now appears at the front, and the time-scale of the novel catches up with itself, as it were. The sixth chapter is then a climax, a long and detailed picture of the horrors of the front itself, at the end of which the company to which Bäumer belongs is reduced further from the 80 of the first chapter (and losses had brought it to this figure from 150) down to 32. This attrition is seen too in detail, as the individuals to whom we have been introduced also fall, one by one.

That sixth chapter is detailed, and marks the end of the first part of the novel; the second part covers a far larger number of experiences, and moves faster towards the end. The action moves away from the front, and Bäumer and two others find a brief consolation in the arms of some French girls, after which Bäumer himself is sent on leave, an experience he finds unnerving, as the experiences of war have cut him off so radically from his earlier life at home. The eighth chapter sees Bäumer faced in a camp with some Russian prisoners of war, one of the few detailed glimpses that we are given of an enemy, and then he returns to an already crumbling front, only to find himself drilling in parade-ground style for a visit by the Kaiser. Sent to the front again, he volunteers for a patrol, and is trapped in a shell-hole with a French poilu, whom he kills with his dagger - a reflex action taken in terror of his own life - and with whom he is left for some time before he can escape to his own lines. This encounter with another enemy who hardly seems to be an enemy prompts frenzied thought and a determination that there must never be another war, but on his return, Bäumer watches a sniper firing, and the chapter ends with an acceptance of the only philosophy which can, in this context, preserve sanity, that war is somehow its own justification, and justifies all other things: "Krieg ist

Krieg schließlich" [p. 198].

The final three chapters move even more swiftly towards the end of the war and the end of Bäumer's life. Moved to a village which has been evacuated "weil es zu stark beschossen wird" [p. 199] the survivors of the little group enjoy a brief period of relative well-being in that they have good food, but are subjected to constant shelling. What is important is that here again what is emphasised is the force of the attack upon them, and indeed, throughout the book the war seems to be of defence against heavy fire, a heavy fire that seems itself not to come from a human enemy, but to be a manifestation of war as an entity in itself. Bäumer is wounded, and brought with one of the others to a hospital, where he has opportunity to observe not the war as such, but at rather more leisure the effects of war on the soldier. Early on in the war postcards were issued by both sides showing the wounded (or even the dying) soldier, and those soldiers would be portrayed typically lying apparently unscathed apart from, say, a clean head-bandage, cradled very frequently in the arms of a pretty nurse.[4] Remarque provides a powerful demythologisation of this when he gives us a more realistic detailing of the various places where a man can be wounded, and the hospital experience sums up the horrors of war, of which death is by no means the worst. "Erst das Lazarett zeigt, was Krieg ist" [p. 221] is one of the most important sentiments in the novel. The conclusion of this tenth chapter typifies the narrative style of the rest of the work. In about half-a-dozen succinct sentences Bäumer is given leave, finds this harder to cope with than before, takes his leave of the friend hospitalised with him, and returns to the front.

The final two chapters are brief and, in contrast to the first part of the work, virtually without detail. We have reached 1918, and the war has resolved itself into an endless attack on the nerves of the surviving soldiers. Most of the others in Bäumer's immediate group are killed, even at the last Katczinsky, the great survivor. As the technology of war gives the upper hand to an enemy whose tanks seem to embody the crushing nature of the war itself, and as the introduction of fresh American troops tips the balance still further, Bäumer can see nothing more than the trenches, disease, death, field hospitals and mass graves. A few lines may sum up the repetitive, sometime anaphoric but essentially expressionist style of these last chapters - they read almost like an August Stramm poem - which are like a musical stretto, bringing fugal motifs together in a condensed form:

---

[4] I have described examples in my *Fighting Songs and Warring Words*, (London, 1990), p. 78.

Granaten, Gasschwaden und Tankflottillen - Zerstampfen, Zerfressen,
Tod.
Ruhr, Grippe, Typhus - Würgen, Verbrennen, Tod. Graben, Lazarett,
Massengrab - mehr Möglichkeiten gibt es nicht. [p. 234]

The final chapter gives Bäumer's thoughts at the very end of the
war. Unable at first to imagine how he could possibly cope in a world
after a war which now seems to be ending after all, he at first despairs,
but at the last he reaches a kind of resigned determination to go on, an
insistence on life in spite of his individual self. His last thoughts are
significant and ironic at once: he will cling to life "mag dieses, das in
mir "Ich" sagt, wollen oder nicht" [p. 241].

The novel has been narrated by Paul Bäumer, and although he has
always spoken in the first person, that first person has been both plural
and singular. His private thoughts, either on the nature of the war, or
when the experiences are concerned with himself alone, as on leave or
in the hospital, have indeed been in the *Ich*-form, but frequently he uses
the *wir*-mode as well, a somewhat flexible first-person plural
standpoint. Usually that *wir* refers to Bäumer's own immediate group,
with a subdivision from time to time between Bäumer and his
classmates, and the wider group which includes Katczinsky, Tjaden and
the rest. Sometimes, of course, it can mean the "Muschkoten", the slang
term used for the ordinary soldiers en masse, and sometimes again it
can even mean the German army as a whole. At the end, though, the
wir has given way to an *Ich*, and even that identity, that individuality as
Bäumer is viewed in a detached fashion. All of the others have been
killed, and at the last, so is Bäumer, and his death, of course, is
presented objectively.

The work is not a memoir; it is a novel, and the reader is
deliberately reminded of this fact at the end. A laconic conclusion tells
us that Bäumer fell in October 1918, at a time, that is, when the fighting
was all but over. The report contains the famous line, now proverbial in
many languages, but ironic in its ambiguity in German. Bäumer's death
is not worth reporting - there is no news on the Western Front worth
speaking of. And the death of a soldier like Bäumer is certainly nothing
new on the Western Front. The conclusion, in an author voice, or at
least, a voice other than that of the rest of the novel, comments that
Bäumer died quickly, and that there was an expression on his face that
looked almost - the word "beinahe" is significant - as if he welcomed
death as an escape from facing a world he could not imagine. Those last
lines also remind us, however, that Bäumer was not an historical figure,
but a fictional one. They serve to draw us suddenly and markedly away

from a fictionality in which we have as readers entered the thoughts and being of Bäumer, and to show us that Bäumer is no more. The ending might be compared with other Weimar war novels in this respect. In Edlef Köppen's *Heeresbericht*, for example, the central figure is still alive at the end of the work, and he has a continued fictional reality in that the reader may wonder what could have become of him after the novel ended. Adrienne Thomas' *Die Katrin wird Soldat* is couched in the form of a diary by the central figure, and although she herself dies at the end of the work, the final comments are by a supposed owner of the diary, so that the fictionality of Katrin's existence is maintained, and she is even referred to in a later novel by the same author. We are not, on the other hand, given a fictive diary by Bäumer, and his thoughts could not have survived in an assumed reality because he himself does not survive. Instead, we are drawn back to the beginning of the work and to Remarque's opening assertion, the all-important preface which allows, and indeed demands, that Bäumer be taken as to some extent as a generalisation, although he is, in fact, clearly an individual. The book, Remarque says, is neither an accusation not a confession, but simply an attempt - again the word "Versuch" is important - to report upon a generation (that of Bäumer and of Remarque himself, of course), which was destroyed by the war even when its members were not killed. The fictitious Paul Bäumer does die.

One does not need to look for Remarque in the novel any more than one needs to make it into an historical documentation. Some of the experiences of Bäumer do match those of Remarque, and his name combines Remarque's own middle name with that of his grandfather, but this has significance neither symbolically (in spite of ingenious attempts to make links with "Baum" and "aufbäumen") nor personally. The fictionality of Paul Bäumer, the nineteen-year old through whose eyes the war is experienced, must be remembered, but so must the fact that Remarque is recreating a view of the war from this particular perspective, that of a young ordinary soldier, and is presenting, selecting (he shows us very little of the actual war, and gives us neither date nor location most of the time) and slanting his narrative at a distance of ten years.

The style of the novel, finally, has clearly contributed towards its lasting popularity. It is easy to read, moves from incident to incident to maintain interest, whilst keeping to a limited range of characters. More to the point, its restriction of the point of view to the lowest level of the army and its avoidance of detailed examinations of historical events as such meant that it could - and can - be transferred to any army. That the

German soldiers in the Lewis Milestone film version speak with American accents makes very little difference. Indeed, it is no accident that the work translated so well into film in 1930, a film which the increasingly powerful Nazi party found sufficiently threatening to want to disrupt the performances in Germany. Those parts of the narrative which describe action are exciting and those which are philosophical are not difficult to grasp, being cast consistently into the thoughts of the young Bäumer. And yet the novel has suffered from a critical approach of a different kind, namely a kind of literary snobbery which demands, perhaps, a more deliberately literary style. This approach - which dismisses the work as 'literary journalism' - ignores the fact that the work makes quite specific demands upon the reader, and is aimed at a readership, as Remarque himself made clear on several occasions, that is deliberately large. The novel had a serious point to make in 1928 and it continues to make a serious point, even if the emphasis has shifted somewhat. It aims, too, to make the point in as forceful a way as possible, and to deny it as a major work of literature is to fall into the trap that Yeats fell into when he excluded the poetry of Wilfred Owen from the *Oxford Book of Modern English Verse* on the grounds that war was not a fit subject for poetry. The approach to Remarque and his most famous novel is beset with such traps.

The publication of *Im Westen nichts Neues* gave rise to a whole range of related publications in German and indeed in English. While many - indeed, most - of the works concerned are of interest only for having been published at all, they do make a kind of collective point. Hyped or not, *Im Westen nichts Neues* had a powerful impact on literary presentations of the war, comparable to, but greater than that of Barbusse and *Le Feu* a decade earlier. Remarque's novel can, in literary terms, serve as a yardstick against which other novels of the war may be measured, and many were directly influenced. Plievier's novel of the navy, *Des Kaisers Kulis*, has been mentioned already, and it resembles Remarque's work in that it presents directly another aspect of the war from a similar perspective, in this case that of the ordinary seaman. But as may be seen in the title, with its relationship between emperor and coolies, there is a rather clearer political bias than in Remarque. So too Adrienne Thomas' *Die Katrin wird Soldat* shows us the war from the point of view of a woman, a Red Cross nurse, who develops the emphasis on the effects of war rather than the fighting, and who dies in the same resigned fashion as Bäumer at the end of the work. There is a similarly pessimistic conclusion in an English work which is based strongly upon Remarque, but again is concerned with women, this time at the front as ambulance drivers. Evadne Price's *Not So Quiet... * picks up the same final resignation in a work which also looks with despair at the post-war prospects for a generation whom the war has ruined for everything.

As part of the marketing of the novel in book form (it had first appeared with some abridgements in the magazine *Vossische Zeitung* in 1928), Ullstein issued a pamphlet with responses to the novel from all kinds of sources, from literary critics to ex-soldiers. The English publisher issued, also as a pamphlet, the correspondence on the novel between Remarque and General Sir Ian Hamilton that had appeared in the magazine *Life and Letters*, Hamilton having been sent a pre-publication version of the translation by A. W. Wheen, a translation which, in spite of the fact that it long established itself as definitive, is in fact not particularly good as a representation of Remarque's original and contains a number of actual errors as well as infelicities. German responses made directly to the novel, however, ranged from simple variations on Remarque's theme to attacks on Remarque himself (such as that by Kropp) or his style (in Salomo Friedländer's *Hat Erich Maria Remarque wirklich gelebt*), down to overtly political condemnations, inspired by the policies of the emerging extreme right. Most of these works are difficult to find, and rarely worth the effort of doing so, having at best a literary-historical value. Two, however, may contribute to an understanding of Remarque's novel: the parody *Vor Troja nichts Neues*, by M. J. Wolff, hiding behind the nom-de-plume of Emil Marius Requark, and a deliberate counter to Remarque by Franz Arthur Klietmann, *Im Westen wohl was Neues*. The first of these uses Remarque's novel as a basis for criticism partly of the adventurous war novel as a money-making enterprise, but it is not really - or at least nor exclusively - anti-Remarque. If there are digs at Remarque's (and Ullstein's) presumed commercialism, the novel also mocks the heroic ideal of war as embodied by Homer, who appears as the official war correspondent at Troy. The link between Paul Bäumer and Homer's completely negatively presented Thersites - a soldier in the *Iliad* who criticises the heroes and who is punished by them - was made early on in criticism, but a twentieth-century response to Thersites might well be more positive than Homer intended. Novels of the First and the Second World Wars frequently draw a contrast between the teaching in schools of a classical and idealistic approach to war, and the realities of a present day war which the pupils then have to face.

Klietmann's attack on Remarque is deliberately conceived *contra Remarque*, and a parody opening statement claims that it precisely *is* an accusation, accusing Remarque, for example, of inflicting a wound upon himself to escape front line service - one of the various rumours spread about him. Its interest, however, lies in the fact that it takes many of the incidents in *Im Westen nichts Neues* and presents them from a different angle. The approach is that of assuming Remarque's novel to be a representation of a series of facts which Remarque has somehow distorted. Thus a group of soldiers - which does not include Bäumer, who is dismissed as a foul-mouthed coward - visit the dying Kemmerich. But it is not Remarque's Kemmerich, but an older, originally more robust character, who dies bravely and nobly. At the end of this incident in Remarque the phrase "eiserne Jugend" is picked up and the word "Jugend" rejected by soldiers whose youth has been stolen from them. In Klietmann's (per-)version, they reject the word "eisern" because they are affected emotionally by the death of their comrade. The same technique is found throughout the work, though the main aim is to present Remarque's incidents as indicating flaws in Bäumer as a single - and not typical - personality, something which might give us food for thought, though not in the way Klietmann intended. The visit to the French girls becomes a nightly visit to the local brothel, the scene with the portable lavatories is a public affront, the food is always excellent, and so on. Klietmann's central figure goes on leave, drinks with the old men, attracts all the girls, and is generally perfectly clear on why he is fighting: to avoid becoming a slave of the French. The work has two overall effects, however, neither, presumably, intended by Klietmann. Some of the scenes of the war itself are so close to those in Remarque that they act as a corroboration rather than a refutation. And very frequently Klietmann's exaggeration becomes almost hysterical, so that any effect he might have wished to make is lost. This is especially clear at the end of the novel - and the war - and here in particular a comparison with his work makes the effect of that by Remarque very clear. The work, it must be remembered, is again a product of the late Weimar Republic. Klietmann's central figure does not die, and nor does his Bäumer. It is significant that Klietmann should deny Bäumer this, and it focusses our attention on the question of why Bäumer dies just before the end of the war. In Klietmann's work, Bäumer becomes a revolutionary, a Bolshevik, upon whom the loss of what Klietmann takes as a perfectly justifiable war of defence can be blamed. Given that the revolution at the end of the war originated in the German navy, Klietmann shows us a hospital with several thousand syphilitic sailors, and takes the line that the sacrifice and bloodshed have been betrayed by a stab in the back -

the "Dolchstoßlegende". Indeed, he even uses the word (with a curiously racist twist as the "Dolchstoß eines Negers") when describing what he calls "dieser schmachvolle Zerfall des eigenen Volks". He blames the defeat on strikes at home, and has associated these attitudes with Bäumer and therefore with Remarque. It is a literary irony that Remarque should be made to carry the blame for Germany's defeat; and an historical tragedy that the views of writers like Klietmann were the ones that prevailed in Germany not long after.[5]

Erich Maria Remarque wrote a sequel to his novel in 1931, one in which he attempted to show the soldiers looking for *Der Weg zurück*, the road back not only to Germany but to life, and here the narrator is almost Paul Bäumer *redivivus* . The work is of very considerable importance to a proper understanding of *Im Westen nichts Neues*, but it is again a pessimistic work, and Remarque was soon forced to leave Germany by the ever more powerful National Socialists, a political refugee in spite of the fact that his books - as he himself stressed, and as many critics have pointed out - are not specifically political, but rather are social in their pacificism. The books, nevertheless, were burned by the Nazis in 1933. Remarque lived in Switzerland until the outbreak of the Second World War, and there wrote *Drei Kameraden*, which appeared in the Netherlands in 1937, and which shows once again the isolation of the war-generation.[6] He moved to America in 1939, and spent his time after the Second World War between America and Switzerland. He died on September 25, 1970 in Locarno with some ten further novels to his credit, some concerned with the Second World War.

---

[5] Franz Arthur Klietmann, *Contra Remarque. Im Westen wohl was Neues*, (Berlin, 1931) has, predictably, not been reprinted. Interestingly, Peter Gay, *Weimar Culture*, (Harmondsworth, 1988), p.144, whilst pointing out that Remarque does not subscribe to the "stab in the back" theory, still considers the novel to show that the men were defeated at the front, something which is also debatable.

[6] Christine Barker and R. W. Last, *Erich Maria Remarque*, (London, 1979) rightly consider *Der Weg zurück* and *Drei Kameraden* in a chapter together, pp. 69-94. *Drei Kameraden* appeared in Amsterdam in 1937, with a translation by A. W. Wheen in Boston in the same year.

Chapter Two

Weder eine Anklage noch ein Bekenntnis:

Approaches, Themes and Point of View

Henri Barbusse's novel *Le Feu* was first published in Paris in 1916 and was translated into English (as *Under Fire*) and German (as *Das Feuer*) in 1917 and 1918 respectively. It was regularly reprinted through the 'twenties and after, although it was banned in Germany during the Third Reich. The novel has as a subtitle "Journal d'une escouade" ("The story of a squad", "Tagebuch einer Korporalschaft"), and it focusses upon a small group of ordinary soldiers caught up in a war, the horrors of which are graphically presented. In a recent study of three French novelists of the First World War a judgement of *Le Feu* appeared which is worth quoting at length, because it raises important questions relating to the approach not only to Barbusse, but to *Im Westen nichts Neues*. Remarque's name and that of his novel might easily be substituted for those of Barbusse and *Le Feu*, and the author, Frank Field, concludes with a reference precisely to the later novel, which was clearly influenced by *Le Feu* in content, style and even structure:

> It must be admitted that, partly because of the haste in which it was written, *Le Feu* is not the kind of book that can greatly impress the present-day reader. Despite the visionary power that the novel still retains, its style seems to be over-emphatic, its characterisation two-dimensional, and its plot difficult to follow. The propagandist element in the novel, an element which becomes particularly prominent in the closing chapters where Barbusse entirely abandons the techniques of Naturalism for a kind of Expressionism, is yet a further factor which helps to explain why it has lost much of its original appeal. Barbusse's contemporaries might have acclaimed *Le Feu* as the first successful attempt to depict the First World War in truthful terms. What strikes the reader of today, however, is the way in which the book combines a great deal of indisputably authentic and realistic detail with passages of undisguised rhetoric, rhetoric which, far from enhancing the impact of the author's message, positively diminishes it.... Like so many other famous denunciations of the miseries of the First World War, in fact like Remarque's *All Quiet on the Western Front* and Ernst Toller's play *Transfiguration*, *Le Feu* now seems to be of mainly historical interest.[1]

[1] Frank Field, *Three French Writers and the Great War*, (Cambridge, 1975), p. 38. See p. 39 on the contemporary success of the novel. The English edition of *Le Feu* was translated by W. Fitzwater Wray for *Everyman's Library* (London and Toronto, repr. 1926 etc.); the German version is by L. von Meyenburg and was published in Zurich. Both translations remain available, although for the most recent German edition (Zurich, 1979 and in paperback, Frankfurt/M., 1986) von Meyenburg's version is reworked by Curt Noch and Paul Schlicht. *Le Feu* was highly thought of by readers as diverse as Wilfred Owen, Arnold Zweig and Lenin.

Some of the points made can indeed be related to Remarque's book. The style is emphatic, some of the characters at least are sketchy and seem without depth; there are frequent passages of rhetoric, and the Naturalist style of some of the work gives way at times to a more concise and telegrammatic style close to that used by the Expressionists. And yet we have to ask ourselves whether the overall judgement stands: certainly Toller's *Die Wandlung* is rarely read. But Remarque's work in German and in translation is still reprinted and read. Is it only of historical value? And has the reception of it changed radically over the years?

Various literary tags may be applied to *Im Westen nichts Neues*. Given that it is set in a clear historical period, "novel of the First World War" is possible, and that would perhaps make it - for the present-day reader - into an historical work, possibly reinforcing Field's viewpoint. Indeed, even when it was written, in 1928, the First World War was already historical, though a large portion of the original audience, like the author, clearly remembered or had participated in it. That audience, too, was German in the first instance, and it is legitimate to ask whether Remarque's novel belongs to German or to world literature. It is, moreover, a product of the Weimar Republic, of a specific point in German history, so that the tag "Weimar novel" is another possibility. Finally, the question arises of whether the simple term "war novel" (or "anti-war novel") is not enough; that is, if the reception of the work today is not merely historical, in Field's sense, then what is the message if the work for the modern reader, given that a war of this kind is no longer likely?

It is appropriate to direct at *Im Westen nichts Neues* a series of questions concerned with the literary presentation of war and of the Great War, to try and see how it tackles them, if indeed it does so at all. The nature of the answers will have a bearing on the three receptive levels of the work: as a picture of the war in 1917-18, as a Weimar novel, and as a work with a longer-term appeal. The most obvious of the questions that can be asked is very simply, what was the First World War like? Others that might seem obvious prove to be less so, in fact, upon closer examination, and they had a particular relevance for Weimar Germany: how did the war begin? Who was responsible for its prolonged continuation (with the extremely important rider of whether those actually fighting bore any responsibility themselves for the war)? Even more complex - though it looks obvious - is the question of whether Germany was defeated. The answers to some of these questions may vary depending on political standpoints, and the extent to which they are answered in any novel of the war will depend upon the point of view from which the narrative is presented. It is appropriate, then, to look not just at the facts of the narrative viewpoint - for the bulk of *Im Westen nichts Neues* consistently that of a nineteen or twenty year old ordinary soldier - but at the effect that the adoption of such a narrative perspective has for the presentation of the war. Here again the three chronological levels of analysis of the novel come into play, of course: the war as it appeared in 1917-8; as it appeared to a Weimar Republic trying to come to terms with its past; and to the modern reader.

It is worth rehearsing the positive or negative possibilities of approach in a novel of the First World War. A positive approach to the war would imply a stress on the view that the war was in some senses acceptable, either because it gave rise to acts of individual heroism, or more broadly and more politically because it represented the rebirth of a German nation in the storm of steel. Such a novel could still admit, or even take as its starting point, the fact that the war was lost, but would either try to explain this (by explicit apportioning of blame, invoking perhaps the so-called "stab in the back", the "Dolchstoßlegende"), or to use it as a call to revenge, to expiation of the shame by a new militarism. This view prevailed historically, and it is possible to understand the attitude of mind that was reluctant to admit that the war was a massive waste of life and nothing more. Before the Nazi assumption of power in 1933 and the banning of all books that took a different view, there were novels which combined anger at the loss with an affirmation of the glory of the men who fought. Josef Magnus Wehner's *Sieben vor Verdun* in 1930 did this, and incidentally placed the blame for the failure to take Verdun on the general, Falkenhayn. The "stab in the back" motif appeared in many guises, with a variety of different dagger-wielders - we have already seen Klietmann's absurd version. After 1933, works like Karl Bartz's *Die Deutschen vor Paris*, a somewhat hysterically-written quasi-historical work (the distinction between such works and novels can be difficult to determine) which sold well in 1934, asked questions about individual aspects of the German loss of the war (the concept "defeat" is less frequently used), as this does of the withdrawal from the Marne in 1914. Its first chapter is entitled "Sieg! Sieg! Und dennoch Rückzug?" and once again it lays blame on the generals.[2] Other battles, though, were taken as symbolic for the birth by fire of a new German spirit, and one of these was Langemarck, one of the few places mentioned in *Im Westen nichts Neues*, when Bäumer replies to the major who stops him when he is home on leave.

---

[2] Karl Bartz, *Die Deutschen vor Paris. Die Marneschlacht*, (Berlin, 1934 - not reprinted), p. 5.

His company is based "zwischen Bixschoote und Langemarck", - on the Flanders front, that is, not far from Ypres. Remarque deliberately does not develop the point, and that is the sole mention of a place, but it is a significant one. It was the scene of fierce fighting on several occasions, in 1915, and also later, in 1917 and 1918, and is the site of the largest of the German military cemeteries. On July 10, 1932 Wehner, for example, produced *Langemarck. Ein Vermächtnis. Worte...zur Stunde der Übernahme des Gefallenen-Friedhofs in Langemarck*, and the place became a symbol of military heroism. Hermann Thimmermann's *Der Sturm auf Langemarck. Von einem, der dabei war* was published in Munich in 1933. Remarque has, of course, nothing of this aspect of Langemarck, and the reference to the place makes it look as if this is deliberate. He has no wish to belittle the fallen, and the place name is a kind of tribute, but it is significant that he does not take it further.

The central character in *Im Westen nichts Neues* and those that we meet through him are in the main naive, and this is historically acceptable. The men who fought in the First World War, and especially those who, like Bäumer, had come to the army straight from school, were given no real reasons for the war, and they themselves can only discuss it in the most general of terms. The novel itself provides an answer to the questions of what a modern war is like, or what it was like to fight on the Western Front. The Weimar war novel, however, was well able to ask other questions that seem naive of themselves, and there is a further set of equally naive questions that relate not to the First World War, but to war as such. Both types of question are reflected in the novel, and if no answers are provided in the text, the impression taken away by the reader is that the second type of question is the more important. The most immediate questions concerning the First World War are very simple: who started the war, and why? In whose interests did it continue? Indeed, did the men fighting have any responsibility for the war as such - a difficult question and one not often asked. For the Weimar Republic, additional questions would include: was Germany defeated, and if so, how? Was there any point to this war? With historical hindsight, the reader in 1928 might have asked in addition how things could have been different, and how such a war could be prevented in the future. And for the modern reader, the questions might be more all-embracing, and thus more difficult to answer except with cynicism: why do nations go to war? Does good ever come out of war?

Other war novels of the Weimar period tackled the historical questions more firmly than *Im Westen nichts Neues*. It is interesting that both Remarque's novel and another work much influenced by it, Theodor Plievier's *Des Kaisers Kulis* quote the well-worn tag:

> Gleiche Löhnung, gleiches Essen
> wär' der Krieg schon längst vergessen ...

which demands equality in the military sphere at least, albeit in a minimal form. Plievier, however, shows us the idea expanded, and the attempt to put it into practice in the abortive revolution in the navy in 1917, after which Köbis and Reichpietsch were executed. Remarque could not show us the historical workings-out of an emergent socialism in fact, but neither does he reflect any aspect of social revolution much beyond the little verse in the discussions of his soldiers. This is not true of other works. Arnold Zweig's *Erziehung vor Verdun* has spokesmen for this point of view who act as unofficial teachers to the central figure of that novel, and even in Ernst Glaeser's *Jahrgang 1902*, in which the central character is younger and more naive than Remarque's soldiers, there is a clearer indictment of what was perceived as being behind the war. Glaeser's central figures are schoolboys, but the father of one spells out in a letter to his son what he sees as the capitalist basis for the war, and it is worth quoting in extenso and comparing with the political awareness of Remarque's men and with the underlying assumptions of *Im Westen nichts Neues*. Glaeser's schoolboys hear the view that those guilty of beginning and of continuing the war are

> 1. die Generale - denn der Krieg ist ihr Handwerk;
> 2. die Minister - denn sie wollen Belgien und Polen haben;
> 3. die großen Unternehmer - denn sie verdienen an ihren Granaten Millionen. Diese drei Typen findest Du in allen Ländern. Deshalb geht der Krieg weiter. Sie haben sehr viele Angestellte, die durch schöne Reden und mit Hilfe einer idealistischen Philosophie das Volk betäuben. Diese Angestellten sind die Pfarrer, die Lehrer, die meisten Redakteure und jene bürgerlichen Dichter, die zu dumm oder zu faul sind, die Wahrheit zu sagen.[3]

The speaker is a socialist who does admit that he himself was taken in by the jingoism of the early years, and the false unity brought about by the outbreak of war in 1914 (and not unknown as a modern phenomenon) is a major theme in Glaeser's book. Remarque shows us that effect only by flashback, of course, since his novel starts in a war that is already stultifying. Some of the indictments made by Glaeser's speaker are there in Remarque too, although socialist critics of the novel criticised it for not making a stand and for not making any of these

---

[3] Ernst Glaeser, *Jahrgang 1902*, (1928), (Berlin, 1986), p. 198.

points overtly. Glaeser's analysis of the blame starts at the top - with the generals and ministers of the crown (and implicitly with the Kaiser, who is explicitly blamed in some other Weimar novels, such as Adrienne Thomas' *Die Katrin wird Soldat*). Remarque's consistent use of one perspective, not just that of the private soldier, but that of a schoolboy turned soldier, leads to the bulk of blame in the novel being placed on teachers, who fall into the category that Glaeser's character calls the *Angestellte*. For Remarque's narrator, the war is to a large extent a *trahison des clercs*; teachers who should have had the intellectual capacity to know better and to see through a crude nationalism purvey it wholesale. The drawing of Kantorek and indeed his final discomfiture when the tables are turned upon him, especially since he is bracketed with an erstwhile janitor, makes its own point, and the message for the Weimar Republic is developed in *Der Weg zurück*. The command system of the army is another enemy, although we do not see as far as the generals, merely a few ranks above private for the most part, with a glimpse and a slight deprecation of Wilhelm II himself. That he appears at all carries the message that this is the Kaiser's war - it is rare for a Weimar novel to exclude him entirely. A far more political work, Theodor Plievier's novel of life in the navy, a work designed as a naval counterpart to Remarque's novel, has the revealing title *Des Kaisers Kulis*, and it draws a clear distinction in class-based terms between the officer caste and the 'coolies', slaves for the emperor, who appears once (the scene is not unlike that in Remarque's work) and makes a speech which virtually no-one can hear. He is mouthing quite literally empty words, and at the end of the novel we are shown the Kaiser fleeing to Holland, claiming that the age of heroic gestures (which he demanded from the men) is past.

Remarque does not comment much on the expansionist aims implied by Glaeser's letter-writer (who is echoing the views of the Independent Social Democratic Party at the start of the war), nor does he make an explicitly class-orientated attack on a repressive officer caste, as does Plievier. He might, of course, have done so. Barbusse's *Le Feu* concludes with an almost mystical vision of a new dawn which condemns the "sword-wavers, the profiteers, and the intriguers ... interested parties ... who live on war" as well as the "savages" who are intoxicated by military music, "the traditionalists, for whom an injustice has legal force because it is perpetuated", the opiate provided by religion, and the many "who befog you with the rigmarole of theory, who declare the inter-antagonism of nationalities at a time when the only unity posessed by each nation of today is in the arbitrary map-

made lines of her frontiers."[4] Barbusse's soldier-voice calls for the
hands of the common men to recognise their real enemies, and to work
together against them not in a war but for international peace. The
ideals of the *Internationale* echo in the passage, it is true, and this kind
of directness in a work which clearly influenced Remarque throws a
light upon Remarque's quite different approach to the same basic
problems of responsibility for the war.

The question arises, though, of whether a simple explanation of the
war was relevant by 1928, or whether it had become an academic
historical point. What was required was indeed far more complex,
something that we might now term "Bewältigung der Vergangenheit".
The German audience in the Weimar Republic needed to come to terms
with the fact that the war had happened, not who began it, and wanted to
know whether or not it had been a complete waste of lives or whether
something - anything - good might have come from it. That point was
not only a German one. The international success of *Im Westen nichts
Neues* and other war novels showed that the deliberately general nature
of Remarque's questioning helped all the combatants to come to terms,
not just the Germans. Another slightly earlier best-seller, Arnold
Zweig's *Der Streit um den Sergeanten Grischa* was acclaimed because,
among other things, it gave such a clear picture of the specifically
German side of the war. That point was made by General Sir Ian
Hamilton and quoted on the dust-jacket of the first English edition, for
example, and very shortly afterwards he was to acclaim Remarque's
work as showing the war from the point of view of the ordinary soldier
in all the armies.

Remarque is not concerned in detail with apportioning guilt for
starting the war. Indeed, few novels of the period in any language
attempt this, something they share with a good many history books.
Perhaps the best historical comment on the causes of the Great War - in
literary terms, at least - remains that provided by two former soldiers
of the war who were no longer able to take seriously a nationalistic
approach to recent history, and thus produced a wonderfully garbled
version. W. C. Sellar and R. J. Yeatman report in *1066 and all That*
how:

> King Edward's new policy of peace was very successful and culminated
> in the Great War to End War... The Great War was between Germany
> and America and was thus fought in Belgium, one of the chief causes

---

[4] Cited from the English translation by Wray (Everyman, 1926), pp. 338-44. The passage as a
whole is of considerable importance to a reading of *Im Westen nichts Neues*, especially on the question
of what constitutes an enemy and on the nature of war. The comment (p. 342) that "the act of slaughter
is always ignoble; sometimes necessary, but always ignoble" is of special interest.

being the murder of the Austrian Duke of Sarajevo by a murderer in Servia.[5]

Many of the Weimar war novels acknowledge the German invasion of Belgium and the annexation policies, but frequently refer also to similar acts by other nations. Others focus upon the assassination in Sarajevo, and though he, too, was writing with historical hindsight, the Austrian writer Stefan Zweig noted in his memoirs that the death of the Archduke was not at the time felt to be so serious. The central figure of Adrienne Thomas' *Die Katrin wird Soldat* notes:

> Traurig genug, daß Österreich mit Serbien Krieg hat. Soviel Blutvergießen um zwei Menschen, die davon doch auch nicht wieder lebendig werden. Na ja, Phantasie haben sie immer gehabt, wenn's sich um Kriegsgründe handelte.[6]

Remarque's criticisms are in fact limited to aspects of the annexation policy and they are not prominent, but they are present. We must recall once again that these are Paul Bäumer's reports of what he hears, and the expression is intended to seem naive, to be consistent with his character (possibly the most important thing to remember throughout the book). It is a deliberately naive view that is being presented, through the eyes of a young man who did not survive to work out the consequences in detail himself. But the fact that he does actually voice such views, and at a fairly late stage in the war, aims them clearly at the Weimar Republic, in which new expansionist policies were already being demanded by some of the parties involved. Bäumer listens during his period of leave as the older men debate the political situation:

> Sie disputieren darüber, was wir annektieren sollen. Der Direktor mit der eisernen Uhrkette will am meisten haben: ganz Belgien, die Kohlengebiete Frankreichs und große Stücke von Rußland[p.156]

The use of a rather different "wir" from the rest of the novel is striking. The Direktor is an authority figure and patriot - he has presumably handed in his gold watch-chain against an iron one in support of the war effort. Remarque might not be making a direct statement about the cause of the war (or perhaps its rationale), but in the stereotype figure of the Direktor the point is being made nevertheless. It

---

[5] *1066 and all That* appeared for the first time shortly after *Im Westen nichts Neues* in 1930, representing a rather different kind of "Vergangenheitsbewältigung". The passage is cited from the 1960 Penguin edition, p. 121.

[6] Adrienne Thomas, *Die Katrin wird Soldat*, (1930, with the same publisher as Remarque's book) (Frankfurt/M., 1987; the latest edition is Munich, 1988 with the same pagination), p. 91. See Stefan Zweig, *The World of Yesterday*, (London, 1943), pp. 167-9, on the deaths at Sarajevo.

is aimed at those elements in the Weimar Republic which would, sadly, soon come to power, but it can also make a general point about the way wars begin, one not necessarily thought through by the soldiers.

Remarque's approach to the war seems radically different from that adopted by, say, Wehner or the other positivist writers, but to see *Im Westen nichts Neues* simply as negative in its approach to the war remains something of an oversimplification. The action of the novel (as opposed to the flashbacks) takes place in the last years of the war, when it had already been lost, but it might be noted that *Im Westen nichts Neues* ends (as did several other Weimar war novels) before November 1918. Bäumer is unable to see how he will be able to cope in a Germany at peace, but there is no room for the specific question of a defeated Germany. This point bears different interpretations, and the fact that the end of the war has not yet come may well say something different to a world after the Second World War than it did to the Weimar Republic.

In 1940 the military correspondent of the London *Times* published a pamphlet which asked the question "Was Germany Defeated in 1918" and did indeed reach the conclusion that the German armies were defeated in the field, commenting that this defeat was

> conditioned by the attrition to which those armies were subjected in 1916 and 1917, and by the exhaustion and loss caused by their own offensive in 1918.[7]

He considered the effect of the blockade to be less significant, and dismissed entirely the notion of the "stab in the back". That idea, voiced by the Kaiser in his own memoirs and widely used in the Nazi period is not even mentioned by Bäumer, and he too plays down the effect of the blockade, even though he does criticise profiteers at home. What is interesting is that Bäumer makes roughly the same point as the 1940 pamphlet, but comes to a different conclusion. The Nazis, in condemning Remarque's book for its "betrayal" of the men who fought at the front, clearly failed to notice that Remarque is, through Bäumer, invariably positive about the soldiers, however negative he is about the war. There are no real cowards, no deserters. Bäumer reaches almost a state of despair as to when the end of the war will come, and he is aware of the constant attrition and of the state of their equipment, but he and those still alive stay at their posts, and the others are still there when the novel ends. There is continuing criticism through Bäumer of the way the war is being prolonged, but in spite of the state of mind reached by Bäumer at the end of the novel, he states quite clearly:

---

[7] Cyril Falls, *Was Germany Defeated in 1918?*, (Oxford Pamphlets on World Affairs 35, 1940), p.6.

> Wir sind nicht geschlagen, denn wir sind als Soldaten besser und
> erfahrener; wir sind einfach von der vielfachen Übermacht zerdrückt
> und zurückgeschoben. [p. 236]

The question of who lost the war is not a clear one, and Remarque
leaves it open. For his Weimar audience this is important as far as the
self-respect of the soldiers is concerned. A post-1945 reading, however,
might place a different interpretation upon the ending. The war does not
end in the novel because it did not end in 1918 or 1919 in any case: it
continued in 1939 and did not end until 1945. By the time he came to
write *Der Weg zurück* Remarque was himself becoming aware that the
Great War did not end wars, as had been claimed, and indeed, the 1930
Nerofilm version of Ernst Johannsen's *Vier von der Infanterie* - filmed
as *Westfront 1918* - places a question-mark after the word "Ende" at the
close of the final reel. As early as 1934 an American documentary was
produced with the title "The First World War".[8]

The lack of overt comments on the beginning, continuation and
indeed ending of the war, and the avoidance of political issues in general
makes Remarque's novel different from those by Plievier, for example,
or indeed from the right-wing novels and quasi-historical writings
where blame for the defeat is attributed. Remarque does touch on many
of the points at issue, but they are not in the foreground, and the work
remains a social, rather than a political novel, addressing two main
themes: the nature (and evils) of modern war itself, and the position of
the young men who went from school to war, whether or not they
escaped the shells. Here the role of the narrator has to be borne in mind,
and the creation and consistent believability of Paul Bäumer is a literary
achievement of very considerable importance. The relationship between
author, narrator and text varies considerably in the Weimar war-novel
(and in comparable writings outside Germany). Thus Ernst Jünger's *In
Stahlgewittern* is presented as a personal memoir, while other works
might reflect the author's own experiences, even though the name of the
central figure is not that of the author. This distancing is clear, say, in a
work like *Die Katrin wird Soldat*, in which Adrienne Thomas uses the
immediacy of a diary, but has it supposedly edited after the death of the
writer by another fictitious character. Ernst Glaeser's *Jahrgang 1902*
has a slightly different problem. The narrator is referred to simply as
"E." and may be identified with the author, but although much of the
work is in the present tense it is clearly an historic present, since there
are sometimes authorial comments which place the work very clearly in
the Weimar period and remind us that the whole thing is retrospective.

[8] See Jay Hyams, *War Movies*, (New York, 1984), pp. 41 and 46.

The Weimar war novel - of which *Im Westen nichts Neues* is still the best-known example - is, of course, always retrospective. It is Remarque's achievement that his narrator (who is, after all, a fiction) never allows us to remember this. Adrienne Thomas' diarist is not so consistent. A seventeen-year old girl is not likely to have written in July 1914:

> Krieg. Und mir ist, als sei es nicht der erste, den ich mitansehen muß, als habe ich schon viele tausend Mal seine verpestete Luft geatmet - geatmet, während Millionen daran in ihrem eigenen Blut ersticken.

or on August 3, 1914:

> Die Versetzung ins Jensseits ist halt leichter als die in die nächste Klasse.[9]

Remarque does not allow Bäumer to step out of his role as a soldier in 1917-8. He is of course not Remarque, and *Im Westen nichts Neues* is not a memoir. Those who took the work, however illogically, as autobiographical, did not pay due attention to the opening statement, which sets the book into a context, as a report of events affecting a particular group (though it of course deals with others), nor the final statement, again by the author-voice, announcing the death of Bäumer. But the bulk of the work is still a presentation of the war through one particular pair of eyes, those of a young and inexperienced man whose thoughts are therefore necessarily naive at times, because they cannot be otherwise. The other characters and events in the novel are seen through his eyes, too, and this may perhaps counter some of the criticisms levelled at the work. The charge of sentimentality in the scene between Bäumer and his dying mother is easily dismissed, and it is in any case hardly trivialised, providing as it does a brief glimpse of the hardships suffered by the poor. The understatement of the mother's illness contrasts, in fact, with the more strident approach to similar scenes in the works of Plievier. A more frequent criticism, however, is that many of the other characters are two-dimensional, but this overlooks the elementary point that a first-person narrative only really ever contains one character - in this case Bäumer. What we see of other characters we see through him; they will be conditioned by his mental processes, and thus they will vary in depth. Those closest to him - Katczinsky most notably - do have a certain amount of depth, but what the reader is shown of them is effectively the way they relate to Bäumer himself. We are given very little of Kat's background, for example, but Bäumer

---

[9] Thomas, *Katrin*, pp. 93 and 96.

would not have experienced this, merely heard of it. That he typifies his schoolfellows as clever, or studious, or his other comrades by their original jobs or by the attributes they have demonstrated in the army, is also understandable, as is the generalised response he has to cook-sergeants and to army doctors. That it is Bäumer's novel and that we have to see the war through his eyes at the time it is happening should not be forgotten.

The kaleidoscopic presentation of a series of different events is also linked with the narrative standpoint, even though the structure of the novel has sometimes been seen as facile and undemanding. In fact it is not: it reflects not only Bäumer's assimilation of a variety of impressions that come upon him at random and sometimes in rapid succession to one another, but it also makes clear his own development of mind. The rapid changes of scene are found mainly in the chapters when he is away from the front at the beginning of the novel; the chapters where he is at the front are more sustained and concentrated, and chapter six is also the longest. The final chapters become increasingly condensed, as his senses become dulled by the seemingly never-ending war. The themes of the earlier parts of the work are reiterated in a more concise form, with ever-new minor variations (such as the gunning-down of two whole companies of new recruits by an airman, acting "aus Spaß", before they have any idea how to find cover), in the two brief final chapters - the last a couple of pages only. Throughout the work, indeed, there are various patterns of alternation, which add to the readability of the work and give a varied picture of the war, but these alternations also shift as the work progresses. There are alternations between periods at and away from the front, between harsh or gruesome and lighter incidents, between action observed by and thoughts within Bäumer. Frequently, however, Bäumer will summarise in a concise and almost Expressionist manner what he has described, and the final chapters of the work as a whole are in themselves a summary of this kind, relating to the whole work -- the best example is the anaphoric section on "Sommer 1918" in the penultimate chapter [p.235].

Far-reaching reflection or hindsight or political comment from Bäumer would constitute just as serious a break in the narrative standpoint as would a gratuitous authorial insertion. Bäumer is an intelligent and reflective young man, but he is all too aware of his limitations. Remarque is at pains to present to his Weimar and to his later audiences an apparently immediate and unretouched picture of the war, so that those audiences (both with the benefit of historical knowledge) may consider for themselves the points that are raised.

Sadly, Weimar and all too often, indeed, subsequent generations, failed to do so.

Chapter Three

Die Front ist ein Käfig:

Paul Bäumer's War

The war happens to Paul Bäumer. He finds himself hurled into it without time to think (the only classmate who shows reluctance is bullied nevertheless into joining up and is killed almost at once). The images he uses for the front line in particular are significant. It is a cage, or a whirlpool, threatening and inescapable. Indeed, war becomes an entity in itself, something outside, a disease; Heinrich Böll placed as a motto to his Second World War novel *Wo warst du, Adam?* a quotation from St-Exupéry's *Flight to Arras* which describes war not only as an ersatz-adventure rather than the real thing, but as a disease, like typhus, and so does Bäumer [p.226]. This is of course linked with the responsibility question, but as far as Bäumer is concerned, war comes from outside himself and imposes its will upon him. War means death, and death is the real enemy. An enemy in the sense of someone fighting on the other side, someone whom Bäumer attacks because he wishes to attack, is not present. We hear of the English or of the French (with an allusion even to black soldiers, probably from Senegal), and of the Americans towards the end, but few enemy soldiers are ever seen, with the exception of Gérard Duval, the French poilu killed by Bäumer as a reflex action in a shell-hole in no-man's-land. It is noteworthy that almost the only French soldier to appear in person is given a name, a trade, even a family - Bäumer finds photographs in his paybook. This all goes towards the contrast between the single incident in which Bäumer is forced to face a real person for a period of time and the picture of the rest of the war, where the enemy is a concept rather than a reality. In the Duval incident, the striking feature is not that Bäumer kills him - he does so as a reflex action, almost - but that he is forced to stay with the man for a period, and is thus confronted because of his enforced proximity to the other man by the humanity of the soldiers on the other side. Normally this is not the case, even though when he tells the story of the incident later Bäumer himself comments that such a happening is "nichts Neues". The killing of Duval is not really even hand-to-hand fighting; the essence here is that it is too swift to admit of human considerations. The men have in general become dangerous animals, surviving themselves only because of their animal instincts:

> Käme dein Vater mit denen drüben, du würdest nicht zaudern, ihm eine
> Granate gegen die Brust zu werfen. [pp.119f.]

The soldiers are not fighting; they are defending themselves from death. There is no recognition of the humanity, let alone the identity of the conceptualised" enemy, and it is this that makes the Duval incident so effective. It is equally noticeable that Bäumer, on his return, is made to watch a sniper at work, and the language is both anonymous and euphemistic, the language of target-shooting, when really it is about killing. Watching him at work brings Bäumer back to what has become normality, and thus to the comfortingly circular thought that "Krieg ist Krieg". The incident persuades Bäumer that the war is not - as it had seemed to him just before - about individuals, and that the Duval incident was an aberration. The First World War was, after all, the first time that refuge could be taken behind the anonymity of the machine. It was the first mechanised war, and it gave the opportunity of dissociation that has been a feature of all subsequent wars. A cartoon during the Vietnam war, for example, showed a bomber in operation, with one man saying, as the bombs fell: "just pretend there's no one down there".[1] There are few visible enemies in *Im Westen nichts Neues* and at the same time the soldiers do not want to be confronted with human enemies, because that forces a different kind of thought. It is well worth noting that one of the rare outspokenly pacifist statements in the work occurs in the Duval scene, with Bäumer's (spoken)

> "Ich versprech es dir, Kamerad. Es darf nie wieder geschehen." [p.196]

The main feature of the physical description of the war is precisely the anonymity, and this, apart from the Duval incident, leads to the soldiers' view of the war as an external and malevolent force against which they are passive, the real essence of which is concealed still further in slang terms. The grammatical forms are revealing:

> Nun aber gab es am letzten Tage bei uns überraschend viel Langrohr
> und dicke Brocken ... [p.42]

> Diese Nacht gibt es Kattun ... [pp.77f., repeated]

All this reinforces the worm's-eye-view approach, and there is no indication in the work of the larger course of the war. It is only by following slight indications of place and time that we may locate the novel on the Flanders front. It is an irony that the armchair strategists

---

[1] The cartoon appeared in *Playboy* in 1971 and is reproduced to illustrate self-persuasion and changes of attitude in P. Mussen and M. Rosenzweig, *Psychology*, (Lexington, 1973), p. 97.

encountered by Bäumer when he returns on leave point out that he as an individual soldier cannot understand the war as such. The whole exchange is of interest. First, Bäumer is instructed that a breakthrough is necessary, to which Bäumer responds

> daß nach unsere Meinung ein Durchbruch unmöglich sei. Die drüben hätten zuviel Reserven. Außerdem wäre der Krieg doch anders, als man sich so denke.

But this is rejected by his interlocutor, who knows better:

> ... es kommt doch auf das Gesamte an. Und das können Sie nicht so beurteilen. Sie sehen nur Ihren kleinen Abschnitt und haben deshalb keine Übersicht ... aber vor allem muß die gegnerische Front in Flandern durchbrochen und dann von oben aufgerollt werden. [p.156]

The irony of the whole is double-edged: Bäumer as an individual soldier can indeed only see his own section of the front, but still he is right and the other man is wrong: Bäumer is aware that a breakthrough is impossible all along the line, and his awareness, based on experience, points up the whole question of strategy. Questions of strategy are not discussed because in the First World War - as was perfectly clear to Remarque and others by 1929 and as had been clear to many soldiers in the war itself - there was very little by way of strategy altogether. It opened with the unsuccessful Schlieffen plan, the pincer strategy proposed by a general who was dead before the war started, and it developed into a war based on the principle of attrition: sheer weight of numbers, it was thought, would prevail. It is, of course, easy to simplify historical details with the benefit of hindsight, but the attitudes of the generals in the First World War was itself simplistic, and as history shows, the years of trench warfare in fact produced few results - no territorial gains for a massive loss of life. For 1917-8, Paul Bäumer's war is an entirely realistic one, borne out by comparable writings, documents and indeed what we have by way of film. Its wastefulness was very much clearer by 1929, but the absence of any political basis, of any military strategy, and the presentation of war as a piece of social, rather than military history, ensures that it has retained its relevance. The First World War remains baffling in its origins and in its conduct, and thereby makes an anti-war point in a general sense that much more clearly.

In some respects, Remarque's presentation of the war is restricted. There are few officers visible, for example, although there are some, and they share in the experiences of the men who are - as they point out themselves - in the vast majority. One cook-sergeant and one corporal-instructor are castigated, though the latter, Himmelstoß, in fact undergoes a change from being transferred to the front, and shares the experiences of ordinary soldiers. A home-based major who adopts a drill-hall attitude to Bäumer when he meets him on leave is implicitly criticised, but beyond that the war is a private's one, a majority war. Other officers are simply not shown. Bäumer himself, however, goes through a range of typical experiences, from initial (and brutal) training to service at the front, from leave to service in a camp for Russians POWs, thus showing him another enemy in human form, although he cannot really grasp that these gentle and defeated souls are really his enemy; then from being wounded to hospitalisation, from hand-to-hand fighting to the more usual passive state of being attacked and defending himself against death itself as woods, villages, graveyards and trenches themselves are destroyed by shellfire. The deliberately long-drawn-out sixth chapter, which is set at the front, allows Bäumer to enumerate all the kinds of bombardment; he does so by presenting a simple list, a technique that Remarque permits him to employ on various occasions. The brief comment attached serves as a summary, and relates to several similar passages later in the work. Here we are shown

> Trommelfeuer, Sperrfeuer, Gardinenfeuer, Minen, Gas, Tanks, Maschinengewehre, Handgranaten - Worte, Worte, aber sie umfassen das Grauen der Welt. [p.133]

Im Westen nichts Neues - like many of the Weimar anti-war novels, and those in other languages as well - systematically demythologises the war, removing a powerful mythology that hovers even around the slight ambiguity in the term "Great War". Various myths arose during the war itself, and were perpetuated actively from the home fronts, and passively to an extent by the soldiers themselves in their reluctance to give full details, either for fear of upsetting, through a reluctance to show weakness, for fear of being disbelieved, or indeed through official proscription. Edlef Köppen sets as the ironic opening motto to his Weimar novel *Heeresbericht* a quotation from the *Oberzensurstelle* in 1915:

> Es ist nicht erwünscht, daß Darstellungen, die größere Abschnitte des Krieges umfassen, von Persönlichkeiten veröffentlicht werden, die nach Maßgabe ihrer Dienststellung und Erfahrung gar nicht imstande gewesen sein können, die Zusammenhänge überall richtig zu erfassen. Die Entstehung einer solchen Literatur würde in weiten Volkskreisen zu ganz einseitiger Beurteilung der Ereignisse führen.[2]

---

[2] Edlef Köppen, *Heeresbericht*, (1930) (Reinbek bei Hamburg, 1979).

By the end of the nineteen-twenties, of course, it was possible to combat the myths by presenting a picture of what the war was actually like, and, indeed, to make quite specific attacks on the way some of the myths were maintained at home. Köppen, in fact, does this systematically in his novel, in which the narrated experiences of a fictitious soldier are juxtaposed with actual documentation, newspaper reports and advertisements which offered a quite unreal picture of the soldiers' life to those at home. Bäumer even comments upon this himself at one point:

> Was in den Kreigszeitungen steht über den goldenen Humor der Truppen, die bereits Tänzchen arrangieren, wenn sie kaum aus dem Trommelfeuer zurück sind, ist großer Quatsch! [p. 138]

The soldiers retain a sense of humour not for its own sake, but "weil wir sonst kaputt gehen", and it is transitory. The propaganda of consistent high spirits in the trenches is a lie: "der Humor ist jeden Monat bitterer".

The principal myth of the First World War was that war itself could still be something heroic, that it could ennoble, and that there was such a thing as a *Heldentod*. Those not actually involved in the fighting were of course unaware that this war was quite unlike the relatively recent Boer War; and the earlier, but already mechanised American Civil War, which might have provided useful lessons, was too far away. The Franco-Prussian War of 1871 was certainly still in living memory, but its course was again very different. Accordingly, behind all the calls to King, Kaiser or country lay a presumption in the popular mind that the soldier was still primarily an individual man of action, able to make the choice of fighting bravely, thereby achieving either death or glory, the former outcome subsuming the latter in any case. Postcards produced by all the combatant countries showed the soldier marching (and indeed sometimes riding) forward, or perhaps making a bayonet charge as an individual; and if - as often - he is shown as wounded or even dying, then this is happening cleanly. Remarque (and others) removed this myth precisely by showing that the soldier was usually in no position to make choices of any description, that he was rarely fighting man against man and that death in battle, far from being a quasi-classical *Heldentod*, was anonymous and agonising, and far more seriously, was not even the worst thing that could happen. Of course the war poets (in English in particular) had made the last point by showing the bitterness of the maimed soldier, but the effect of Remarque's novel is cumulative. It is always worth recalling the very obvious: that the common denominator of all wars is that they are predicated upon people being killed or maimed. In the relatively brief description of hand-to-hand fighting in chapter six soldiers are bayonetted in the back or have their faces smashed with a trenching-tool.

There are no heroic deaths in *Im Westen nichts Neues*, and this was the basis of one of the criticisms levelled against it. Indeed, it cannot be denied that the First World War did give opportunity for acts of individual heroism (though the massive scale of carnage can hardly be justified for that reason, as the proponents of the *Stahlbad* view of the war tried). Remarque, however, shows us death first in terms of broad attrition - Bäumer's company has been reduced from one hundred and fifty to eighty men when the novel opens, and by the end of chapter six there are thirty-two left. We hear of (and sometimes are shown), more specifically, the loss of Bäumer's classmates, and we see in detail in the final chapters of the novel in particular (some, like Haie Westhus, are killed earlier on) the gradual loss of Bäumer's immediate group - a group composed of former classmates and others befriended in the army, and to whom we have been introduced in the course of the novel. The deaths are presented objectively, with few comments (and those sometimes ironic), and the pointlessness of the whole war is made clear. What is made clear is the lack of grounds for any of the individual deaths, as indeed for the attrition which happens outside the novel. No ground is won, no victories are claimed, and some of the deaths are literally accidents of war.

> Müller ist tot. Man hat ihm aus nächster Nähe eine Leuchtkugel in den Magen geschossen. Er lebte noch eine halbe Stunde bei vollem Verstande und furchtbaren Schmerzen. [p. 231]

> Der gleiche Splitter hat noch die Kraft, Leer die Hüfte aufzureißen. Leer stohnt und stemmt sich auf die Arme, er verblutet rasch, niemand kann ihm helfen ... Was nützt es ihm nun, daß er in der Schule ein so guter Mathematiker war. [p. 235]

Bäumer carries the wounded Katczinsky back for medical treatment, but on the way he is hit again:

> Kat hat, ohne daß ich es gemerkt habe, unterwegs einen Splitter in den Kopf bekommen. Nur ein kleines Loch ist da, es muß ein ganz geringer, verirrter Splitter gewesen sein. Aber er hat ausgereicht. Kat ist tot. [p. 239]

Other deaths described are as graphic, but are not linked with individuals. One one occasion "zwei werden so zerschmettert, daß Tjaden meint, man könne sie mit dem Löffel von der Grabenwand abkratzen" [p. 130]. In another case a death is presented in some detail but without our ever seeing the dying soldier. Under fire, Bäumer reports that the wounded can usually be rescued from no-man's-land, but this is not always the case. Sometimes they simply have to listen to men dying:

> Einen suchen wir vergeblich zwei Tage hindurch. Er muß auf dem Bauche liegen und sich nicht umdrehen können. Anders ist es nicht zu erklären, daß wir ihn nicht finden ...

The soldiers analyse without expressed emotion what is wrong:

> Kat meint, er hätte entweder eine Beckenzertrümmerung oder einen Wirbelsäulenschuß. Die Brust sei nicht verletzt, sonst besäße er nicht so viel Kraft zum Schreien ... [p. 127]

The cries last for days, but the man cannot be found. Inducements are offered to anyone who can find him, but Bäumer comments that the promise of additional leave is hardly necessary, since the man's cries can hardly be borne. He is never found, but Bäumer and his fellows can follow every stage of the man's death, from his cries for help to his conversation in delirium with his wife and children, to his final and long-drawn-out death throes. The description takes up several full paragraphs, and the soldier himself is seen neither by the reader nor indeed by those in the novel. The repetition of horrible and anonymous death is a feature of the novel, and indeed, even after death the soldiers are not safe from the war. Two passages remain in the mind. One of the most famous passages in the novel, in the fourth chapter, shows us the soldiers under fire, and Bäumer and his colleagues find themselves in a recently established military burial ground; ironically, Bäumer has to take cover in a grave that has been opened up by the shellfire and disgorged its occupant, leaving the living soldier to shield himself from death by death:

> ich krieche nur noch tiefer unter den Sarg, er soll mich schützen, und wenn der Tod selber in ihm liegt. [p. 87] [3]

A counterpart to this comes in the central sixth chapter, just after the passage described already in which an unknown soldier dies so slowly.

---

[3] Paul Fussell, *The Great War and Modern Memory*, (Oxford, 1975), p. 196 describes the scene as a Gothic fantasia and embroiders it somewhat: "the narrator and his chums preserve themselves by crawling into the coffins and covering themselves with stinking cerements." He also refers to the place as a "civilian cemetery." All this misrepresents the book fairly thoroughly (it is quite specifically a military cemetery and a recent one at that, there are no cerements unless we count a brief reference to "Tuch", and only Bäumer's position is described).

Here, the dead cannot be retrieved, and are indeed buried by the shellfire; the description is again unemotionally laconic, and quite uncompromising:

> Die Tage sind heiß, und die Toten liegen unbeerdigt. Wir können sie nicht alle holen, wir wissen nicht, wohin wir mit ihnen sollen. Sie werden von den Granaten beerdigt. Manchen treiben die Bäuche auf wie Ballons. Sie zischen, rülpsen und bewegen sich. Das Gas rumort in ihnen. [p. 128]

In Bäumer's war, however, death is not the worst: "Erst das Lazarett zeigt, was Krieg ist." [p. 221] The novel takes us into the front-line hospital in the very first chapter of the work, to the bed of the dying Kemmerich, who has had a leg amputated. Kemmerich lives long enough for us to see the waste of a young life, of a young man who could now no longer fulfill his ambition of becoming a forester even were he to survive. But he will not survive. All the while the reader is reminded of the stench of carbolic, pus and sweat, and it is significant that Kemmerich does not die until the second chapter, when Bäumer again sits by his bedside in the suffocating atmosphere, waiting for his classmate to die. His thoughts link the recurrent idea of lost youth with the despair of waste; his despairing wish that the whole world should be led past the bedside is of course what Remarque effectively does, showing the readers for the first time in the novel a detail not of war, but of the real result of war. Even the history books do not always make clear that the results of war mean people dying as well as countries conquering:

> Franz Kemmerich sah beim Baden klein und schmal aus wie ein Kind. Da liegt er nun, weshalb nur? Man sollte die ganze Welt an diesem Bette vorbeifuhren und sagen: Das ist Franz Kemmerich, neunzehneinhalb Jahre alt, er will nicht sterben. Laßt ihn nicht sterben! [p. 61]

Bäumer has just been thinking of how young and un-soldierly they all look when out of uniform, and here again he reminds us that this is not the heroic death of a professional soldier, but of a civilian who has been bullied or has been forced by circumstances or by history into a uniform. Critics of the novel who miss any explicit pacifism in the novel have failed to notice too, perhaps, the clear message of that "weshalb nur?"

A far fuller presentation of the results of war is found towards the end of the novel when Bäumer himself is wounded and finds himself in a hospital, taken there on a hospital train in which, with irony once again, he is mortally (tödlich) embarassed when he has to explain to a nurse his need to go to the lavatory. The experience of the hospital itself, however leads him to the realisation that here is where the realities of war become clear. The point was made during and after the war, of course, in many places; Siegfried Sassoon's "Does it Matter?" and many poems by Wilfred Owen ("Disabled," "Mental Cases," "The Chances," "A Terre") make the point, but it needed reiterating by the end of the nineteen-twenties. A. M. Frey's *Die Pflasterkästen* and Adrienne Thomas' *Die Katrin wird Soldat* both expand the point made so clearly by Bäumer, but not only does Remarque allow Bäumer to experience the hospital, with some quasi-comic incidents to lighten an effect which might otherwise become unbearable, he also has him enumerate the effects of war:

> Im Stockwerk tiefer liegen Bauch- und Rückenmarkschüsse, Kopfschüsse und beiderseitig Amputierte. Rechts im Flügel Kieferschüsse, Gaskranke, Nasen-, Ohren- und Halsschüsse. Links im Flügel Blinde und Lungenschüsse, Beckenschüsse, Gelenkschüsse, Nierenschüsse, Hodenschüsse, Magenschüsse. Man sieht hier erst, wo ein Mensch überall getroffen werden kann. [p. 220]

The generalising comment following the piling-up of different kinds of wounds is not yet an overt criticism, but Bäumer in fact goes on to describe in more detail still further effects of war - deaths through tetanus, shattered limbs the seriousness of which is made clear to him when he is shown x-ray photographs - and all this leads him to his conclusion, not only that the hospital makes clear what war is about, but that

> dies nur ein einziges Lazarett [ist], nur eine einzige Station - es gibt Hunderttausende in Frankreich, Hunderttausende in Rußland.

And it is this thought which leads the fictitious soldier Bäumer close to private despair in 1918, with a statement that made clear to the Weimar audience that the Great War had been a massive waste of life and that a new war would be the same, and to later audiences that war in general is to be condemned:

> Wie sinnlos ist alles, was je geschrieben, getan, gedacht wurde, wenn so etwas möglich ist? Es muß alles gelogen und belanglos sein, wenn die Kultur von Jahrtausenden nicht einmal verhindern konnte, daß diese Ströme von Blut vergossen wurden, daß diese Kerker der Qualen zu Hunderttausenden existieren. [p. 221]

The word "Kultur" is a key one; the war was described - on British medals - as "the Great War for Civilisation", and in German, emphasis

action, a state upon which military life always depends, even if here the bonding sometimes works against the very forces that have inculcated that fellowship. The communal attack on Himmelstoß is a case in point here, it is only a single incident and it has another more important significance than the expression of comradeship: it is the first expression of the violent solution of war having its reflection in the application of violent solutions to personal rather than national problems, a demonstration of what might be called original sin in man the war-maker. Bäumer, it is true, refers to comradeship as the best thing to come out of the war [p. 59], but the comment has to be treated carefully. He has been talking about a feeling of solidarity engendered in the recruits whilst undergoing initial training, and developed in the field of battle. All this modifies the concept, and in any case, it is determined and conditioned by the war. Comradeship may be the best thing the war produced, but its temporary existence scarcely justifies the war. Indeed, throughout the novel it is not comradeship which is stressed, but loss: the gradual loss of all the classmates and friends. Comradeship in war is only one side of things; the other is the necessity of parting. Bäumer's use of the pronoun "wir" rarely implies a genuine closeness of relationship. An example of parting which is commented upon comes at the end of the hospitalisation scene, when Bäumer and Kropp have to part:

> Der Abschied von meinem Freunde Albert Kropp ist schwer. Aber man lernt das beim Kommiß mit der Zeit. [p. 225]

Only with Katzcinsky does Bäumer share a close relationship, and this is the product of chance rather than of a general comradeship born out of the war. Their relationship is close, but it is almost that of a father and a son. Kat the father-figure (something made clear in both film versions, incidentally), teaches Bäumer to survive, quite literally in the instructions about the different kinds of shell, and more generally in his ability to find food under adverse conditions; and survival against the real enemy - death - is a key theme, the one thing these schoolboy soldiers learn, and which replaces all the learning they have so pointlessly assimilated at school.

What really binds Bäumer and Kat is their lust for life, the fact that they are "zwei winzige Funken Leben" [p. 107] in the storm of chaos about them. And yet they both die. Bäumer's comments on comradeship are in fact developed at the end of the work, and here he links it with the solidarity felt by prisoners or the community feeling of those condemned to death:

> Wir sind Soldaten und erst später auf eine sonderbare und verschämte
> Weise noch Einzelmenschen. [p. 226]

The comradeship is not an absolute; it depends - like the communal "wir" - upon their being soldiers. Take this away, and it is only natural that the feeling of community should go as well. It is no accident that Bäumer should in his last thoughts refer to his identity as an individual. War is concerned with the premature and abrupt killing of many individuals, and Bäumer, like all men, dies alone. Part of the message of the novel is that the war was not fought by the masses, by some kind of numerical abstract, but by huge numbers of individual soldiers. Much of the effect of the work depends on the fact that Bäumer is really the only character, and that it is very much his war. Of course, his experiences were not unique, and as far as action goes, Remarque allows his characters to draw attention from time to time to the uniformity of the war; under fire in chapter six during the 1917 Ypres campaign, Kat comments that "es wird wie an der Somme" [p. 113] a year earlier. Many of the things that Bäumer goes through, sees, feels or thinks will have been known by real soldiers in the war (because Bäumer is, after all, a fictitious character). He himself is an individual, though, and that individuality should not be lost sight of: it expresses itself in his youthful sensitivity in showing us Bäumer's war, and Remarque's skill in making him do so in such a consistently convincing manner is considerable.

Chapter Four

Krieg ist Krieg schließlich

Some Open Questions

Bäumer's fellow soldiers debate at one point the way in which the First World War began, and this develops quickly into a general discussion of how wars start. Their apparently naive comments - naive only in an overt sense, and in fact more sophisticated than they seem in the first instance, and very much along the lines of the child's question of whether the emperor is wearing any clothes - can be applied to any war. That the debate comes just after the Kaiser's visit gives force to the questioning in historical terms, as well as providing a starting-point. The discussion may be once again taken on different levels, however, representative of the way the novel as a whole makes it effect. The debate forms part of the narrative reality for the First World War in the consistent presentation of the unintellectual or merely young soldiers; it has an importance for the Weimar Republic in which the prospect of a new war (designed for the far right, at least, to eradicate the shame of the lost Great War) was already looming; and for the modern reader, the application of these *faux-naif* views to war as a concept makes a pacifist point, reducing the idea of war to an absurdity. The debate contains, though it does not outline in detail, the spirit of internationalism voiced at the end of *Le Feu*. The discussion moves swiftly from the Kaiser himself to the straightforward "wie eigentlich ein Krieg entstehe". The question is subjected to a rhetorical development in that possible responses are tested one after another. Wars are large-scale disputes, not private ones, so that they arise when one country insults another. The technique of absurd literalism applied to this statement questions how a mountain can insult another mountain, say, so that a new definition has to be reached, and the word "Land" is replaced by "Volk". Here the word is taken as embracing quite literally once more all the people of a given country, and since those present do not feel insulted, the concept is again rejected. "Volk" is now replaced by "Staat", and at this point additional elements are introduced; Tjaden rejects the concept because it implies an apparatus of officialdom which is inherently suspect, at least to the ordinary soldier. Katczinsky makes a further distinction, this time between "Staat" and "Heimat", admitting that the latter cannot exist without the support of the former, but in fact refining the definition of "Staat" to mean simply "Regierung". The kind of government controlling a given state at any time can and does cause war - be it an imperial caste-rule, or in Weimar a potentially right-wing extremist government committed to a *Stahlhelm-* philosophy, annexationist, and intent on avenging what was felt to be a shameful defeat.

Bäumer has, in fact, already come to and expressed his own conclusions earlier, during his encounter with the Russian prisoners of war: an anonymous command has begun the war. He does not spell out where the command comes from, but it is a command nevertheless which makes one group of people into enemies on what can look like a quite capricious basis. The most cursory study of shifting alliances even in recent international politics make clear that Remarque's narrator's point has lost none of its force:

> Ein Befehl hat diese stillen Gestalten zu unsern Feinden gemacht ...

The use of the distributive pronoun is significant again in the light of what is meant by "wir" in other parts of the novel (and it is no accident that one of the grammatical questions that have become so unimportant in another discussion between the soldiers is the nice distinction between "wir Deutsche" and "wir Deutschen".) More seriously, and a point picked up again in *Der Weg zurück,* is that the same directive commands the soldier to kill:

> jahrelang ist unser höchstes Ziel das, worauf sonst die Verachtung der Welt und ihre höchste Strafe ruht. [p. 174]

War is very clearly being equated not just with killing, but with murder. Wherever the emphasis of intent in the novel may have lain in 1929 (on the motif of the lost generation, say), the implications that have ensured the continued survival of *Im Westen nichts Neues* as a major novel, and which are indeed designed to do so by their deliberate non-specificity, are those that speak against war as such. It is no accident that Bäumer breaks off quite deliberately his thoughts on war provoked by the Russian prisoners: "Dieser Weg geht in den Abgrund." Certainly for Bäumer self-preservation dictated that he should not pursue a line of thought that could only lead to madness (as indeed it does in some of the war novels, such as Edlef Köppen's *Heeresbericht* or A. M. Frey's *Die Pflasterkästen* .) In the later discussion, too, the debate shifts to the somewhat different question of those for whom the war is an advantage, before breaking down into a deliberate decision not to think about it: "Besser ist, über den ganzen Kram nicht zu reden", because once again, that way madness lies, or did for the soldiers in the Great War. What might have been best in 1917, however, is a signal for the later reader, in the Weimar Republic as now, precisely to ponder on the points raised by Bäumer and others.

Other novels make more specific the question of who was able to use the First World War to advantage, or indeed who were able to live well whilst others suffered. Once again the would-be naivety of the debate between the soldiers in Remarque's novel generalises the point. If Theodor Plievier wrote historical documentary novels of the war - one is entitled *Der Kaiser ging, die Generäle blieben* - Remarque's references are far less specific. There is a general voicing of the notion that military commanders achieve extra glory from wars. So, Bäumer himself mentions later, do the factory-owners (by which is clearly meant those making munitions). The war is fuelled, too, by propagandists on both sides. All these points, however, refer to the continuation of the war, rather than to the reasons behind it. They are symptoms, rather than causes.

The question of personal responsibility is rather different from that of guilt, and more pertinent, perhaps, to the aim of overcoming the past. Plievier in *Der Kaisers Kulis* tackles this question head-on at the beginning of his work, by showing how a group of merchant seamen are shanghaied (thus the title of his first chapter) into the *Kriegsmarine*. They are able to state quite explicitly, therefore, that they had no choice in the matter, and thus they are outside the question of responsibility. Yet wars are fought by people, and in fact Plievier's sailors all refuse to fight at the end - in the naval mutiny which took place at about the same time as the fictional Bäumer is killed on the Western Front. Other novels of the Weimar Republic concerned with the war, too, take all responsibility away from the central figures, going beyond even the question of conscription, which was a kind of exoneration in itself. The heroes of *Die Pflasterkästen* are non-combatants, the narrator of *Jahrgang 1902* too young to fight, that of Adrienne Thomas' *Die Katrin wird Soldat* a nurse. Remarque's soldiers, however, do volunteer, as did so many. They do so, if the chronology is worked through, in 1916, however, rather than as part of the initial euphoria, and the fighting experienced in the novel is in 1917 in the battle known in English as "Third Ypres". The euphoria of 1914 is observed by the central figures both of Glaeser's and of Adrienne Thomas' novels, and in the latter Katrin's male classmates join up with enormous enthusiasm, looking for action and excitement in a war that they think is going to be over in a matter of weeks. They and she are soon disillusioned by the stalemate of the trenches, but Remarque's figures do not belong to that first generation of soldiers. The charge of enthusiasm, of the so-called *Hurrahpatriotismus* that was typical at least at the beginning of the war, cannot be laid at their door. They volunteer, it is true, but they are blackmailed into doing so by their teachers and even by their parents. Kantorek, like other teachers, churns out a standard patriotism which leads the boys to enlist, and Behm, reluctant at first, is one of the first to fall, blinded, left in no-man's-land and then killed. Bäumer specifically - but employing the *faux-naif* approach that recurs in the book - dissociates this death from Kantorek:

> Man kann Kantorek natürlich nicht damit in Zusammenhang bringen: - wo bliebe die Welt sonst, wenn man das schon Schuld nennen wollte. Es gab ja Tausende von Kantoreks, die alle überzeugt waren, auf eine für sie bequeme Weise das Beste zu tun. [p. 49]

There is, then, only the slightest attempt in fact to take away any of the responsibility from Kantorek and from the teachers as a whole, influential people in the world of the schoolboy protagonists, who should have known better. The denial that their action constitutes guilt is at once overturned, and the final statement makes three separate points: that there were countless teachers like Kantorek; that they were acting through (wrong-headed) conviction; and that they were taking good care of their own safety. The accusation is in fact quite clear: the older men at home sent the young to fight their fight. Bäumer is quite specific on the role of the teachers, viewed from the point of view of 1917 - the opening chapters take place after an assault, and Bäumer is reflecting on the past. They are morally bankrupt, but they carried on writing and talking, while the soldiers themselves saw the gunfire and the hospitals. It may be that other groups are implied in this context, but Bäumer does not mention (perhaps because he has no experience of) other potentially guilty parties - the clergy, popular writers, for example - although there is a reference to "Professoren und Pastöre und Zeitungen" [p. 181]. Instead he considers the reality of war and attacks another myth: that the state is an absolute concept, and is all-important. We may recall, too, that even the parents are seen as having played a part:

> mit dem Wort "feige" waren um diese Zeit sogar die Eltern rasch bei der Hand. Die Menschen hatten eben alle keine Ahnung von dem, was kam.
> [p. 48]

But the attack is not quite as savage as that on the teachers, even though Bäumer goes on to say that the war was accepted by the middle classes, who should have had a better idea of what might happen, while it was seen as a misery by the poor. *Im Westen nichts Neues* is, as is clear from the prefatory statement, concerned, too, with one generation, but that generation sees itself as free of the responsibility for the war, and places the blame firmly on the generation before. The question to which Remarque does not address himself is: were the soldiers at all responsible? Could they not have stopped the war? After all, the sailors mutinied, abortively in 1917 and effectively in 1918? It is interesting that Remarque has Bäumer link mutiny with desertion and indeed with cowardice, in a passage referring to a time after the soldiers have learned that what they had been told was wrong:

> während sie [the teachers] den Dienst am Staate als das Größte bezeichneten, wußten wir bereits, daß die Todesangst stärker ist. Wir wurden darum keine Meuterer, keine Deserteure, keine Feiglinge - alle diese Ausdrücke waren ihnen ja so leicht zur Hand - wir liebten unsere Heimat genauso wie sie, und wir gingen bei jedem Angriff mutig vor; - aber wir unterschieden jetzt, wir hatten mit einem Male sehen gelernt.
>
> [p. 49]

The conclusion reached is virtually an existential one; the old world-order preached to them for so long had been found wanting, and they were now as a generation alone, their externally imposed "Schicksal" [p. 102] being to come to terms with things as best they might. One thing that they learned, of course, was the effect of violence, or of the effect that it could have. Placed into a world ruled by violence, where brutality has become an end in itself, rather than a means to achieve something, the soldiers adopt the same attitude, perhaps unconsciously, as in the beating-up of Himmelstoß. In Arnold Zweig's important novel of 1932, *Erziehung vor Verdun*, the "education" implied in the title includes the pessimistic point that one of the central figures, a lieutenant whose brother has been deliberately kept at the front until he is killed, applies precisely the same technique to the person responsible. That violence can become a way of life is another of the points picked up in *Der Weg zurück*.

The question remains of why the soldiers, having become aware of their real situation, carried on. Historically, of course, they did not desert or mutiny, although for the modern reader that might have been interpreted not as cowardice but as bravery, and Plievier dedicated his novel *Des Kaisers Kulis* to the memory of Köbis and Reichpietsch, executed for naval mutiny in 1917. Indeed, a memoir, which appeared in 1928, by one of the mutineers who was pardoned, Hans Beckers, discusses precisely the question of cowardice on his own part in the light of the stand taken by those who were shot. In a foreword to the work, addressed to a future historian "in the year 1991", Tucholsky makes a point about the abortive and ill-planned Wilhelmshaven mutiny of 1917 which refers also to the soldiers:

> Noch nicht der Hunderste von ihnen wußte, wie man eine wirkliche Revolution inszeniert. Aber sie hatten Mut - viel, viel mehr Mut als die ausgelaugte und niedergekämpfte Landtruppe, die nicht einmal das gewagt hätte.[1]

This may contain its own answer: by 1917, the point at which revolution should have come, the land troops - Bäumer amongst them - were as exhausted as their weapons. The sailors' revolt in 1917 may have been ineffectual (as that in 1918 was not), but as Tucholsky goes on to point out, for the German mind and its inbuilt acceptance of authority it was an enormous amount. Unlike many of the Weimar war novels, Remarque does not make clear the role of the Kaiser or see the war as specifically his, although the soldiers do express surprise at his small stature when he comes to distribute medals. Rather he allows his soldiers to answer the question of why they carried on fighting with a kind of generalised patriotism:

> Das Nationalgefühl des Muschkoten besteht darin, daß er hier ist.
> [p.183]

Remarque repeated the point in a broader sense in his letter to Sir Ian Hamilton. The main point about the questioning of the war is that the question is not asked, and indeed, the soldiers did not mutiny. The question - and this too was made clear in the letter to Sir Ian Hamilton - was really directed at those who survived the war and yet in 1928 were still defeated, enervated, lethargic. For Weimar, the reduction of unanswered questions to a refusal to continue talking about them - "wird ja auch nicht anders dadurch" [p. 183] - which may have sufficed in 1917-8, was once again *faux-naif*, designed to draw attention to a state of mind that might recur. For the modern reader, it draws attention to a kind of patriotism: to parody a celebrated, if still enigmatic statement made during the First World War, the modern audience may wonder if this sort of unreflective patriotism is ever enough.

The novel does, nevertheless, address directly the question of the effect of war upon morality in general, and it makes clear the way in which war reverses peacetime standards. This again is linked with the motifs of teaching and learning on the one hand, and with that of killing on the other. All that the soldiers have learnt prior to the war is proved to be useless and is mocked as such; and throughout the novel the

[1] Hans Beckers, *Wie ich zum Tode verurteilt wurde*, (1928), (Frankfurt/M., 1986). See p. 84 and for Tucholsky's comment, the introduction, p. 7.

soldiers are unable to kill when they want to (lice, rats, wounded horses, fatally wounded comrades in agony) but have to kill men they do not hate - a motif that is developed in *Der Weg zurück*. The morality of killing, however, is raised, however, in Bäumer's thoughts - referred to already - when he confronts the Russian prisoners of war. An anonymous command has made these people - whom he does not hate - into enemies, although they do not look like enemies. The anonymous command (the random reversability of which is made clear) is another example of the way in which the war works upon Bäumer. The neutrality of the whole thing ("irgendein..." "einige Leute") generalises the thought, and removes it from a reference to the First World War alone: normally, killing is murder and is punished; but when someone - and someone unknown - signs an equally obscure piece of paper somewhere, then murder is actually sanctioned. But the war introduced weapons that both sides considered immoral when they were first used: flamethrowers and gas are both described in the text. We have seen that Bäumer himself is unable to pursue further the logic of this reversal of morality: that way madness lies. But he resolves to preserve the thought for future use, to return to it after the war. Bäumer does not return, but Remarque's audience, in 1929 as in the present, are clearly invited to think about the pacifist point. Bäumer is a soldier, and does not go on to voice the absolute that Katrin notes in her diary in Adrienne Thomas' novel after she has been to a Synagogue in September 1914:

> Als die Thorarollen herumgetragen wurden, drängten sich die Feldgrauen, die zehn Gebote mit dem Gebettuch zu berühren, um es dann ehrfurchtig an die Lippen zu führen. Auch euer Gott wird euch nicht helfen; für viele unter euch ist es zum letztenmal. Du sollst nicht töten.[2]

---

[2] Thomas, *Katrin*, p. 141.

Chapter Five

Ohne Erwartung und ohne Furcht

The Lost Generation and the Road Back

Im Westen nichts Neues covers in its description the latter part of the war, but there are also flashbacks, and it is not entirely clear when the central figures actually joined the army. Since they went in as part of the general enthusiasm for war - and we are told that even their parents were at that time free with the word "coward" - it has to be assumed that they joined, say, in 1916 at the latest. It is difficult to put a date on the turning point of the war, but perhaps the fateful July 1, 1916, the first day of the bloodshed on the Somme is as good as any. But the linear action of the novel - excluding, that is, the flashbacks - covers the period only from about August 1917 ("Third Ypres" began on July 31), embraces the period in which the tank moved from being viewed as a cumbersome experiment, as it was on the Somme, to a feared weapon, as at Cambrai in November 1917, and continues through the stalemate of 1918 until Bäumer's death not long before the Armistice. It is a documentation, then, of a lost war: it begins with heavy losses and attrition, and ends with the death of the central figure, with Bäumer the last survivor from his group, awaiting peace or revolution. The last chapter of the work is very brief - the shortest of all, two pages only, and a summary of thoughts that are all of Bäumer, who is by now completely isolated mentally, thrown in upon himself, unable to think past the end of the war. He does, it is true, look back at the same time as looking onward:

> Wären wir 1916 heimgekommen, wir hätten aus dem Schmerz unserer Erlebnisse einen Sturm entfesselt. Wenn wir jetzt zurückkehren, sind wir müde, zerfallen, ausgebrannt, wurzellos und ohne Hoffnung. Wir werden uns nicht mehr zurechtfinden können. [p. 240]

The use of "wir" in the context of 1916 refers presumably to the German army as a whole, but in the next sentence the first person plural means all the soldiers who have gone straight from school into the army, and who have therefore missed the opportunity to grow up normally. "Der Krieg" says Bäumer "hat uns für alles verdorben." They are simply not fitted for anything, and they have no aims. He

distinguishes his generation from those who had already begun to settle
themselves before the war, who can return to their old positions and
families, and from those who are growing up after the war, similar to
them, but without their experiences, who will push them aside. The
feeling might be described as justifiable self-pity, and of course it refers
here to a very large group of soldiers. We might add that those who
could have gone back and resumed their old positions after the war
might have included Katczinsky and Detering, the first dead, the second
presumably shot after his apparent desertion, and a work like Glaeser's
Jahrgang 1902 makes a very different point about the next group, young
people affected by the war even though they did not fight. But Bäumer's
view was not uncommon, nor was it incomprehensible; but he is
simplifying and generalising, something done too by Evadne Price in
her novel *Not So Quiet...* in which her protagonist (a woman ambulance
driver) foresees her generation as "a race apart, we war products ...
feared by the old ones and resented by the young ones ... a race of men
bodily maimed and of women mentally maimed."[1] Bäumer is somewhat
more introspective, and somewhat less extreme, but equally pessimistic:

> Wir sind überflüssig für uns selbst ...

At the last, however, he is positive. He sees nature reviving itself, and
feels its power:

> Es kann nicht sein, daß es fort ist, das Weiche, das unser Blut unruhig
> macht ... die tausend Gesichter der Zukunft, die Melodie aus Träumen
> und Büchern, das Rauschen und die Ahnung von Frauen, es kann nicht
> sein, daß es untergegangen ist in Trommelfeuer, Verzweiflung und
> Mannschaftsbordells.

Bäumer becomes calm and draws strength from these thoughts at the
end. Life can take nothing more from him:

> ich bin so allein und so ohne Erwartung, daß ich ihnen [den Jahren]
> entgegensehen kann ohne Furcht. Das Leben, das mich durch diese
> Jahre trug, ist noch in meinen Händen und Augen. Ob ich es
> überwunden habe, weiß ich nicht. Aber so lange es da ist, wird es sich
> seinen Weg suchen, mag dieses, das in mir "Ich" sagt, wollen oder
> nicht. [pp. 240f.]

Bäumer has discovered an identity, his "Ich" has asserted itself at the
end of the war, a war in which he has thought - and has indeed been

---

[1] Evadne Price (writing as "Helen Zenna Smith", the name of the narrator of the work), "*Not So
Quiet ...*" *Stepdaughters of War*, (London. n.d. [1930]), pp. 167-70. The whole section is very like
Remarque, as might be expected from the title.

forced to think - primarily in terms of "wir". But it is too late: Bäumer is killed, pointlessly, at the end, when his death is not even reported, because it is so commonplace and because the death of a private soldier does not merit comment.

Why does Bäumer die? Or rather: why does Remarque permit his central figure to be killed at the very end of the war, commenting then in the voice of an omniscient narrator that Bäumer's face had "einen so gefaßten Ausdruck, als wäre er beinahe zufrieden damit, daß es so gekommen war" [p. 242]? Bäumer does not have to face life after the war, even though he was at the deepest level now prepared to do so, and this is seen as a relief. Bäumer's death in *Im Westen nichts Neues* is the final image of the recurrent motif of the lost generation, the motif that Remarque felt to be the most important when the novel was written, although it had not yet acquired its force in 1918 and it has lost it since. The work, it will be recalled, is dedicated in a prefatory motto that is, like the last paragraph, not by the fictitious Bäumer, to "eine Generation, die vom Kriege gestört wurde - auch wenn sie seinen Granaten entkam" [p. 40]. Throughout the work the motif recurs, and it is bound up with the equally recurrent idea of the robbery of youth even though the soldiers are still young in years - "wir sind keine Jugend mehr" - and the resultant inability of the soldiers to contemplate being able to do anything except be soldiers. Faced with a new world of adult life, they are made to turn their guns onto it. Bäumer's thoughts continue:

> Wir waren achtzehn Jahre und begannen die Welt und das Dasein zu lieben; wir mußten darauf schießen. Die erste Granate, die einschlug, traf in unser Herz. [p. 102]

Such thoughts are frequent in the work. Although Bäumer's despair is expressed most clearly at the end, it is present equally clearly in earlier chapters:

> Wir sind verlassen wir Kinder und erfahren wie alte Leute, wir sind roh und traurig und oberflächlich - ich glaube, wir sind verloren. [p.126]

If the war has spoiled everything for them, it has spoiled them for any useful trade after the war. They have learned nothing but killing.

When it was first published, *Im Westen nichts Neues* was aimed at one lost generation, the Bäumers who did return. Clearly it found a response, even though the concept of the lost or deprived generation has been applied to other groups before and since; arguably most generations in the present century have felt themselves betrayed. At an increasing chronological distance from the events described and from the writing of the novel, when the generation in question is all but gone, not the effects of (the) war on one generation, but the potential effects of war as such achieve primary importance. For all that, Remarque's sequel to *Im Westen nichts Neues* remains of considerable importance to the understanding of the novel. *Der Weg zurück* was less successful, and as was pointed out at an early stage, is far more a German novel than a world novel,[2] but read in conjunction with *Im Westen nichts Neues* it can throw a great deal of light onto the earlier work.[3] Indeed, Remarque himself seems to have been aware of the necessity of a new novel that would clarify some of the points in the earlier work. It is illuminating, too, to compare the endings of the two works.

The narrator of the second work is Ernst Birkholz, who is extremely like Bäumer (to whom there is a passing reference at the beginning). The work is again a first-person narrative, but on this occasion Remarque does on a few occasions move into the omniscient author mode by presenting incidents at which Birkholz is not actually present. The novel opens at the end of the war - a few men are still killed - but there is no comment on the reasons behind the peace, or indeed on Versailles later. Some of the political events of Germany's confused history at the end of the war are reflected, but the concentration is upon the men returning, who do not themselves understand what is going on. Thus there is a confrontation with one of the left-wing worker-and-soldier units which figure so prominently in the writings of Plievier, and which the extreme right saw as dealing the stab in the back to the army, but the narrator and his immediate group do not treat this in political terms. They defend one of their number, who is a lieutenant, and therefore under attack as an officer, but their appeal is to the comradeship in adversity between themselves and one of the soldiers who now forms part of the left-wing group. Although the point is made in *Im Westen nichts Neues* that the officers were more the enemy of the ordinary soldier than those in the opposing trenches, Remarque does not develop that point in the way that, say, Plievier does in *Des Kaisers Kulis*, and here, too, no political point is made. Remarque is more concerned to show the reader the folly of erstwhile comrades turning

[2] Kurt Tucholsky wrote a review of "Der neue Remarque" in May 1931 and made the point: see his *Gesammelte Werke*, ed. M. Gerold-Tucholsky and Fritz Raddatz, vol. IX (Reinbek bei Hamburg, 1975), p. 209. M. Eksteins, *Rites of Spring*, (London, New York etc., 1989), p. 283 notes that Remarque wrote his new novel to clarify the question of the lost generation. It is perhaps this concentration that has restricted the later novel, although it, too, is of importance as a war novel. First published in 1931, there are recent paperback editions, including the Ullstein text (Berlin,1979) cited here.

[3] I have discussed various aspects of *Der Weg zurück* in the introduction to my edition of *Im Westen nichts Neues* and in my talk on the work recorded for the series *Exeter Tapes*.

their guns on one another. Once again the criticism of the book is social, rather than political, but once again it is all very much a commentary on the historical events of 1914-1918. The idea of comradeship in general, already seen as temporary in *Im Westen nichts Neues*, breaks down in *Der Weg zurück* as some ex-soldiers do well and others suffer hardship. The young narrator - Bäumer's contemporary, and representative of the generation Remarque saw as ruined by the war - has difficulty reaffirming his relationship with his family, and in forming new relationships. In this novel, Remarque addresses himself also to the problem of the older ex-soldiers, of whom Bäumer so glibly assumed that they would simply return to their jobs and families. One of Birkholz's fellow-soldiers returns to a wife who has, he discovers, been unfaithful, and this causes a total breakdown in his life, as he moves away from the farm into the town in order to start afresh. The motif of killing and the linked theme of too readily resorting to violence (which crops up on several occasions) returns when an ex-soldier shoots a man he finds with his girlfriend, and then does not understand in court why he cannot kill someone he hates, when he has spent several years killing those he does not hate. The narrator also visits an erstwhile sniper, precisely similar to the one observed by Bäumer after his return from no-man's-land, and in this incident Remarque allows his new narrator, who survived the war, to take up a point that Bäumer could not take up at the time. But he questions the morality of the sniper in vain.

The role of the teachers in placing ideas into the heads of the impressionable young, finally, is given a full treatment. The returning soldiers object to the words spoken at a memorial service by the school headmaster about how

> einundzwanzig Helden ruhen in fremder Erde aus vom Klirren der Schlacht und schlummern den ewigen Schlaf unterm grünen Rasen ...

The word "Klirren" is inappropriate enough, and the notion of dead heroes slumbering under the green grass is as comforting a myth, almost, as some of the postcards of the wounded soldier during the war itself. It was a prettification which was easy to use at ten years' distance in the Weimar Republic,[4] and Remarque swiftly has one of his protagonists demolish the idea. The effect is precisely the same as in *Im Westen nichts Neues*; Remarque's ex-soldier will allow none of the tidying-up of historical fact that could (and indeed did) allow people to forget the war enough to embark upon another. Birkholz's friend Willy literally bellows a retort to those who are still purveying such cant, and

---

[4] Barker and Last, *Remarque*, p. 75.

Remarque is clearly shouting it at those who took the same line in the late Weimar Republic, but it has a universal validity here as well:

> Im Trichterdreck liegen sie, kaputtgeschossen, zerissen, im Sumpf versackt ... Heldentod! Wollen Sie wissen wie der kleine Hoyer gestorben ist? Den ganzen Tag hat er im Drahtverhau gelegen und geschrien, und die Därme hingen ihn wie Makkaroni aus dem Bauch. Dann hat ihm ein Sprengstück die Finger weggerissen und zwei Stunden später einen Fetzen vom Bein, und er hat immer noch gelebt und versucht, sich mit der anderen Hand die Därme reinzustopfen, und schließlich abends war er fertig. Als wir dann herankonnten nachts, war er durchlochert wie ein Reibeisen. Erzählen Sie doch seiner Mutter, wie er gestorben ist, wenn Sie Courage haben.[5]

It is clear from this passage that the message of *Im Westen nichts Neues* is still being stated, and indeed, *Der Weg zurück* is very much a novel of the First World War. As in the earlier novel there is no question of belittling the efforts of the soldiers who fought and were killed in the war. It is the war itself that is at fault. The soldier described died bravely, and if he cannot slumber under the greensward it is because his death was unnecessary and barbaric.

Although the returned soldiers can make this kind of protest to their own teachers, it is debatable what effect it has, other than cowing the older men temporarily. On the other hand, their experiences make it difficult for them to teach others, and it is in this point that *Der Weg zurück* is perhaps most strictly a novel addressed to a Weimar audience about a lost generation. The narrator becomes a teacher, and in spite of a clear fondness for the children, is unable to teach them for long, because the war keeps intruding into his consciousness, a war that the young children in his charge know nothing about. Thus in an elementary writing lesson to illustrate the letter K, Birkholz suggests the word "Kemmel", which baffles the child, who knows nothing of the fighting around Kemmel Hill, near Ypres. He and his colleagues, too, observe the young, the next generation quite literally playing soldiers at the end of the work, chanting "Front Heil!" and accusing Birkholz and his colleagues, including the redoubtable Willy of being "Feiglinge" and "Bolschewisten". Not only is the comment of another of the ex-soldiers significant - "so geht es wieder los" - but so is the fact that on this occasion there is no clear victory for Birkholz and his fellows. The young would-be soldiers and their leader (the word "Führer" is used throughout for the man in charge) simply move away. Their time will come. Remarque makes clear with the incident that the lessons of the war that he has tried to put over in his two novels have not been

---

[5] *Der Weg zurück*, p. 71.

learned.

Der Weg zurück remains a novel of the First World War, just like *Im Westen nichts Neues*. Paul Bäumer had said at the end of the earlier novel:

> einige werden sich anpassen, andere sich fügen, und viele werden ratlos sein ... [p. 241]

and this is demonstrated in *Der Weg zurück*. We are shown cripples, men maimed by the war, men whose minds have been destroyed, as well as those who come to terms and exploit the new world. Two, however, commit suicide: first, the lieutenant, ostensibly because he has syphilis, but in fact because the real disease is the war, which is still in his blood. He sees, too, the way things are going already in 1919, and comments on how the next age-group, the seventeen-year-olds, are already joining the right-wing Freikorps and committing political murders. He sees already the road which led to the Third Reich. Secondly, another soldier who finds himself unable to cope, quite literally returns to the front, to the graves of the fallen, and (in a passage which is narrated objectively and given extra prominence thereby) shoots himself. These two deaths, together with the killing and trial, and the visit to the sniper, all come at the end of the novel. The incident with the boys playing soldiers - the boys of 1919 who would accept, by 1933, the new nationalist mythology and their interpretation of the First World War rather than Remarque's - is in a separate "Ausgang". Paul Bäumer had reached a point of almost complete despair, but drew a kind of strength at the end of the novel from the renewal of nature, and was able to shake off some of his desperate melancholy, a melancholy which, although individual, is so much more firmly grounded than the romantic agony of other literary individuals from Werther onwards. The choice of the word "Schwermut" is not without significance, nor - in the light of the Russian romantics and their concept of the 'superfluous man' in society - is the word "überflüssig", although Bäumer does say that they are "überflüssig für uns selbst". Indeed, some critics of the novel have censured Bäumer fairly severely for indulging an adolescent self-pity, a point of view which, even if not wholly acceptable, nevertheless gives cause to think of him as an individual. In fact, Bäumer is able to return to a kind of robust belief in the self which makes his pointless death all the more ironic:

> Aber vielleicht ist auch alles dieses, was ich denke, nur Schwermut und Bestürzung, die fortstaubt, wenn ich unter den Pappeln stehe und dem Rauschen ihrer Blätter lausche. [p. 241]

Bäumer dies, and cannot test this, but Birkholz and his friends are alive. The ending of the sequel, however, makes the same point. The resourceful Willy puts the point into a practical context, and the voice is surely Remarque's in both of the novels as the question of patriotism is picked up again:

> Ich will meinen Jungens da beibringen, was wirklich ihr Vaterland ist. Ihre Heimat nämlich, und nicht eine politische Partei. Ihre Heimat aber sind Bäume, Äcker, Erde und keine großmäulige Schlagworte.[6]

The implications for the dying Weimar Republic and the empty slogans of National Socialism are unmistakable, but the sentiments have a general relevance. Birkholz is not so resolute, but he too draws strength from nature. At the end he is as alone with his thoughts as Bäumer was, but he is alive, and aware that he will have to struggle hard to carry on. Nature and the spring bring him hope. But history has overtaken the novel - indeed, it did so within a year of its appearance - and the reader is returned to the thought that Bäumer, perhaps, was the more fortunate of the two narrators.

Nevertheless, the second novel forms a very important pendant to the first, and although much of it refers specifically to German history at the end of the war, and alludes to the German situation in 1931, it, too, makes points which have a general validity, and they expand for the most part upon the various motifs in *Im Westen nichts Neues* that apply to war as much as to the Great War.

The three interpretational levels on which *Im Westen nichts Neues* must be read are interlinked, and they are of equal importance. The work can be read as a picture of the First World War as it was - it has been taken, after all, virtually as a contemporary report by many critics. Many of the incidents and a great deal of the mood can be verified at least as potentially historical, but various points need to be borne in mind. All history is selective, even when it is intended as history, and the view offered by *Im Westen nichts Neues* is deliberately a restricted one, the war as seen from the point of view of one observant and reflective, but nevertheless young private soldier. But *Im Westen nichts Neues* is not intended as history. It is a novel, and however vivid and immediate it might be, it is still a work of fiction with one fictitious character only through whom the reader sees everything else. In some respects Bäumer may be assumed to be typical of others, but this assumption must not be made too readily: Bäumer is an individual, even though he has been made to conform, both at school

---

[6] *Der Weg zurück,* p. 188.

and more so in the army. Because he is so consistently presented, it is easy to forget that the novel is not a study of the First World War as such, to forget that it is about Paul Bäumer's war, and to forget, indeed, that we are dealing with a novel.

Far from being a contemporary documentation, it is a novel written with authorial hindsight, at a distance of ten years, even if it may be compared with novels of the period of the war itself, such as *Le Feu*. More to the point, it is a novel written with foresight, and it can be related on the second interpretational level to the Weimar Republic, a "Bewältigung der Vergangenheit" which is at the same time a warning of the dangers of unreflective nationalism, patriotism, militarism. It is also an explanation of how the generation that was reaching full maturity in the late 1920s had had the greatest emotional difficulties in coming to terms with the post-war world because they had had their youth taken away from them. Empathy is possible, of course, and this is one reason why the novel remains an important one for young people to read. But while this may have been the primary thrust of the work when it was written, such an interpretation is now of necessity historical. The generation destroyed by the war are now all gone, and as Remarque is honest enough to make clear in the sequel, the war affected many more than the generation born in the last years of the nineteenth century. And beside Bäumer and Birkholz there are the figures of Oellrich and Bruno, the snipers in each of the novels, treating the killing of men just like target practice, and clinging to the notion of war as a justification in itself. Their parts in the novels are small, but eventually they outnumbered the more sensitive equivalents of Bäumer, Birkholz and indeed Remarque.

The third level of interpretation is linked with the second, and the views of the First World War put out by the Third Reich, and the events leading up to and including the Second World War, to say nothing of the increasingly highly mechanised wars since that time, maintain our interest in the work even though trench warfare is a thing of the past. There are plenty of comparisons to be made, and a variety of obvious points can still be made: that war is about killing, whether it is done at a distance or not, and that there is a difference between listening to tunes of glory and fighting for survival against death itself. By presenting us with a sympathetic central figure with whom it is not difficult to identify, Remarque's stated aim of reaching as wide an audience as possible has continued to be valid. By presenting the First World War not as an historical event, but for the most part as war itself, unspecified in place and almost so in time, the novel remains a pacifist one.

Bäumer's "es darf nie wieder geschehen" to the poilu Duval was impossible to act upon in the middle of a war, and indeed, Bäumer's own thoughts of pacificism - brought to life only within the war - nearly lead him to madness. And although it was a message that the Weimar Republic might have heeded, those who burned Remarque's novel in May, 1933 rejected it. It has not lost its validity, however much it may have been ignored. Had Remarque adopted in his novel a specifically political approach, it might have been less successful. Certainly a work like Plievier's *Des Kaisers Kulis* has not had the same success, and that, too, adopts a worm's-eye-view approach. Remarque's novel is social, rather than political, but there is still an irony in the whole work that is expressed in the title, and that refers to class. To be sure, officers also died; but the private soldiers, the "Muschkoten", the poor bloody infantry, were in the majority. The work does speak for the majority, and it is noticeable that when Remarque allows his soldiers to reach this internationalist conclusion, the reference is to both sides, and to civilian occupations:

> Aber bedenk mal, daß wir fast alle einfache Leute sind. Und in Frankreich sind die meisten Menschen doch auch Arbeiter, Handwerker oder kleine Beamte. Weshalb soll nun wohl ein französischer Schlosser oder Schuhmacher uns angreifen wollen? [p. 182]

The First World War was the first to involve civilian soldiers on a massive scale, and the first to contain mechanised warfare on the same scale, the first time that war had become the monster that the German Expressionist poets saw it as. The real victim of war, though, is the ordinary soldier, and we are returned to the irony of the title. Bäumer's death was nothing new, and therefore was not news. The same point was made in 1861 in the context of another war, in a poem on the death of a single sentry:

> 'Tis nothing, a private or two now and then
> Will not count in the news of the battle.[7]

The poem, "All Quiet Along the Potomac", may have contributed towards the English title of Remarque's novel. Remarque, however, is not concerned with the news of the battle, but with the importance of the death of the single unimportant private soldier.

---

[7] Ethel Lynn Beers, "All Quiet along the Potomac" in: *Songs of the Civil War*, ed. Irwin Silber, (New York, 1960), pp. 128-30.

SUGGESTIONS FOR FURTHER READING

This bibliography concentrates on *Im Westen nichts Neues* as a work of literature. Most histories of the First World War are excluded, as are most of Remarque's other works and the secondary works concerned with them, reference works, books of pupils' notes on the text (there are several), and all but a few of the many general studies of the novels of the war. On the other hand, a list - though by no means one that is remotely exhaustive - of some comparable (anti-)war novels is provided, to help place Remarque into a broader literary context; many of these works have been reprinted, some frequently, and often in paperback. Poems, plays, letters and most diaries are omitted, however, as for the most part are positive militaristic writings and adventure-stories of the war. The many contemporary responses to, attacks on, and parodies of *Im Westen nichts Neues* are hard to come by even in libraries, and their interest lies in the main not in what they contain, but in the fact that they were published at all; works like *Hat Erich Maria Remarque wirklich gelebt* are accordingly not listed.

PRIMARY

Erich Maria Remarque, *Im Westen nichts Neues*, (Berlin, 1929, repr. 1988 etc.); with added documentation, ed. Tilman Westphalen (Cologne, 1987); ed. Brian Murdoch (London, 1984, repr. 1988). *All Quiet on the Western Front*, tr. A. W. Wheen (London, 1929, many reprs., most recently 1990); new tr. with an afterword Brian Murdoch (London, 1994).

Erich Maria Remarque, *Der Weg zurück* (Berlin, 1931, repr. 1979; Cologne, 1971). *The Road Back*, tr. A. W. Wheen (London, 1936, repr. 1979).

Erich Maria Remarque, *Drei Kameraden* (Amsterdam, 1937). *Three Comrades*, tr. A. W. Wheen (Boston, 1937).

Ian Hamilton and E. M. Remarque, "The End of War? Correspondence", *Life and Letters*, 3 (1929), 399-411. Also in J. Glover and J. Silkin, *The Penguin Book of First World War Prose*, (Harmondsworth, 1990), pp. 604-10. It was also issued as a 13-page pamphlet by Putnams as publicity material for the book itself.

SOME SECONDARY MATERIAL ON REMARQUE AND *IM WESTEN NICHTS NEUES*

Alfred Antkowiak, *Erich Maria Remarque. Sein Leben und Werk*, (Berlin, 1983).

A. F. Bance, "*Im Westen nichts Neues*: A Bestseller in Context", *Modern Language Review*, 72 (1977), 359-73.

Christine R. Barker and Rex W. Last, *Erich Maria Remarque*, (London, 1979).

Franz Baumer, *Erich Maria Remarque*, (Berlin, 1976).

Kathleen Devine, "The Way Back: Alun Lewis and Remarque", *Anglia*, 103 (1985), 320-335.

Axel Eggebrecht, "Gespräch mit Remarque", *Die literarische Welt*, 5/24 (June 14, 1929), 1-2.

Modris Eksteins, *Rites of Spring. The Great War and the Birth of the Modern Age*, (London, New York etc., 1989), pp. 277-299.

Richard Arthur Firda, *Erich Maria Remarque. A Thematic Analysis of his Novels*, (New York, Berne etc., 1988), pp. 29-64.

Michael Gollbach, *Die Wiederkehr des Weltkrieges in der Literatur. Zu den Frontromanen der späten zwanziger Jahre*, (Kronberg, 1978), pp. 42-83.

Claude W. Hoffmann, "Erich Maria Remarque" in *Dictionary of Literary Biography 56: German Fiction Writers 1914-1945*, ed. James Hardin, (Detroit, 1987), pp. 222-241.

Peter Horn, "Der 'unbeschreibliche' Krieg und sein fragmentierter Erzähler. Zu Remarques Kriegsroman *Im Westen nichts Neues*", *Heinrich-Mann-Jahrbuch*, 4 (1986), 85-108.

Armin Kerker, "Zwischen Innerlichkeit und Nacktkultur. Der unbekannte Remarque", *Die Horen*, Winter 1973, pp. 3-23.

Holger M. Klein, "Dazwischen Niemandsland: *Im Westen nichts Neues* and *Her Privates We*" in *Großbritannien und Deutschland. Festschrift für John W. Bourke*, ed. Ortwin Kuhn, (Munich, 1974), pp. 487-512.

Manfred Kuxdorf, "Mynona versus Remarque, Tucholsky, Mann and Others: Not So Quiet on the Literary Front" in *The First World War in German Narrative Prose (Festschrift George Wallis Field)*, ed. Charles N. Genno and Heinz Wetzel, (Toronto etc., 1980), pp. 71-92.

Rex Last, "The 'Castration' of Erich Maria Remarque", *Quinquereme*, 2 (1979), 10-22.

Helmut Liedloff, "Two War Novels. A Critical Comparison", *Revue de la littérature comparée*, 42 (1968), 390-406.

Richard Littlejohns, "Der Krieg hat uns für alles verdorben: the Real Theme of *Im Westen nichts Neues*", *Modern Languages*, 70 (1989), 89-94.

Hans-Harald Müller, *Der Krieg und die Schriftsteller. Der Kriegsroman der Weimarer Republik*, (Stuttgart, 1986), pp. 60-93.

Brian Murdoch, "Erich Maria Remarque: *Im Westen nichts Neues*", *Exeter Tapes*, (Exeter 1987).

Brian Murdoch, "All Quiet on the Trojan Front: Remarque, Homer and War as the Targets of Literary Parody", *German Life and Letters*, 43 (1989/90), 49-61.

Brian Murdoch, "Translating the Western Front: A. W. Wheen and E. M. Remarque", *Antiquarian Books Monthly Review*, 18 (1991), 452 - 60..

Brian Murdoch, "Hinter die Kulissen des Krieges sehen: Adrienne Thomas, Evadne Price - and E. M. Remarque", *Forum*, 27 (1992), 56 - 74.

Brian Murdoch, "Narrative Strategies in Remarque's *Im Westen nichts Neues*", *New German Studies*, 17 (1992 - 93), 175 - 202.

C. R. Owen, *Erich Maria Remarque. A Critical Bio-Bibliography*, (Amsterdam, 1984).

William K. Pfeiler, *War and the German Mind. The Testimony of Men of Fiction who Fought at the Front*, (New York, 1941, repr. 1966), pp. 140-52.

Erich Maria Remarque zum 70. Geburtsag am 22. Juni 1968, (Cologne, 1968).

Brian Rowley, "Journalism into Fiction: Erich Maria Remarque, *Im Westen nichts Neues*" in *The First World War in Fiction*, ed. Holger M. Klein, (London, 1976), pp. 101-111.

Helmut Rüter, *Remarque: "Im Westen nichts neues". Ein Bestseller der Kriegsliteratur im Kontext*, (Paderborn etc., 1980).

Bärbel Schrader, *Der Fall Remarque: Im Westen nichts Neues: eine Dokumentation*, (Leipzig, 1992).

Wilhelm J. Schwarz, *War and the Mind of Germany*, I, (Frankfurt/M., 1975), pp. 17-70.

Harley U. Taylor, *Erich Maria Remarque. A Literary and Film Biography*, (New York, Berne etc., 1988).

Martin Travers, *German Novels on the First World War and their Ideological Implications, 1918-1933*, (Stuttgart, 1982), pp. 83-105.

Tilman Westphalen, ed. *Erich Maria Remarque 1898-1970*, (Bramsche, 1988) .

Tilman Westphalen, Annegret Tietzeck, Detlef Vornkahl and Josef Wennemer, *Erich Maria Remarque. Bibliographie: Quellen, Materialien, Dokumente*, 2. vols. (Osnabruck, 1988).

SOME GENERAL STUDIES

Peter Aichinger, *The American Soldier in Fiction, 1880-1963: A History of Attitudes Towards Warfare and the Military Establishment*, (Ames, Iowa, 1975).

Bernard Bergonzi, *Heroes' Twilight. A Study of the Literature of the Great War*, 2. ed., (London, 1980).

Alfredo Bonadeo, "War and Degradation: Gleanings from the Literature of the Great War", *Comparative Literature Studies*, 21 (1984), 409-33.

J. K. Bostock, *Some Well-Known German War-Novels, 1914-1930*, (Oxford, 1931).

Paul Fussell, *The Great War and Modern Memory*, (New York and London, 1975).

M. S. Greicus, *Prose Writers of World War I*, (London, 1973).

Helmut Gruber, "'Neue Sachlichkeit' and the World War", *German Life and Letters*, 20 (1966/7), 138-49.

Holger M. Klein (ed.), *The First World War in Fiction*, (London, 1976).

Eric J. Leed, *No Man's Land. Combat and Identity in World War I*, (Cambridge, 1979).

Viktor Neuburg, *A Guide to the Western Front*, (Harmondsworth, 1988).

George A. Panichas (ed.), *Promise of Greatness. The War of 1914-1918*, (London, 1968).

George Parfitt, *Fiction of the First World War. A Study*, (London, 1988)

William Rose, "The Spirit of Revolt in German Literature, 1914-1930" in his *Men, Myths and Movements in German Literature*, (London, 1931), pp. 245-72.

Wolfgang Rothe (ed.), *Die deutsche Literatur in der Weimarer Republik*, (Stuttgart, 1974).

Margrit Stickelberger-Eder, *Aufbruch 1914. Kriegsromane der späten Weimarer Republik*, (Zurich and Munich, 1983).

Robert Wohl, *The Generation of 1914*, (London, 1980).

SELECTED COMPARABLE NOVELS OF THE FIRST WORLD WAR

Jon Glover and Jon Silkin (eds.), *The Penguin Book of First World War Prose*, (Harmondsworth, 1990) [Brief extracts from a wide range of novels from various languages].

Werner Klose (ed.), *Deutsche Kriegsliteratur zu zwei Weltkriegen*, (Stuttgart, 1984). [Brief extracts from German novels].

Richard Aldington, *Death of a Hero*, (London, 1929; unexp. repr. 1965).

Enid Bagnold, *A Diary Without Dates*, (London, 1918; repr. 1978).

Henri Barbusse, *Le Feu*, (Paris, 1916); tr. W. Fitzwater Wray as *Under Fire*, (London and Toronto, 1917). Many reprints of both versions.

Vicente Blasco Ibañez, *Los cuatro jinetes del Apocalipsis*, (Valencia, 1916); tr. Charlotte Brewster Jordan as *The Four Horsemen of the Apocalypse*, (New York, 1918). Many reprints of both versions.

Edmund Blunden, *Undertones of War*, (London, 1928; Harmondsworth, 1982 etc.).

Vera Brittain, *Testament of Youth*, (London, 1933; repr. 1978 etc.).

e. e. cummings, *The Enormous Room*, (New York 1922); intro. by Robert Graves (London, 1928); new intro. by the author (London, 1978).

Roland Dorgèles, *Les croix de bois*, (Paris, 1919 and many reprs.); tr. as *Wooden Crosses*, (London, 1920) [R. Lecavelé].

John Dos Passos, *Three Soldiers*, (New York, 1921; Harmondsworth, 1990).
Timothy Findlay, *The Wars*, (Toronto, 1977; Harmondsworth, 1978) [A modern novel of the First World War].

Walter Flex, *Der Wanderer zwischen beiden Welten. Ein Kriegserlebnis*, (Munich, 1917); Nachwort by. Martin Flex, (Munich [1924] etc.).

Rudolf Frank, *Der Schädel des Negerhäuptlings Makaua*, (Potsdam, 1931); as: *Der Junge, der seinen Geburtstag vergaß*, (1983); tr. Patricia Crampton as *No Hero for the Kaiser*, (New York, 1986).

Alexander Moritz Frey, *Die Pflasterkästen. Ein Feldsanitätsroman*, (Berlin, 1929); Nachwort by. Herbert Greiner-Mai, (Leipzig and Weimar, 1984; repr. Frankfurt/M., 1986); tr. L. W. Charley as *The Crossbearers. A Story of the Medical Corps*, (New York, 1930).

Ernst Glaeser, *Jahrgang 1902*, (Berlin, 1929 [in fact 1928]; Königsstein/T, 1978; Frankfurt/M., 1986); tr. Willa and Edwin Muir as *Class of 1902*, (New York and also London, 1929).

Robert Graves, *Goodbye to All That*, (London, 1929, repr. Harmondsworth, 1961 etc.).

Jaroslav Hasek, *The Good Soldier Schweik*, tr. Paul Selver (Harmondsworth, 1951 etc.) [Czech, 1922; abridged transl. 1930; full German tr. by Grete Reiner, Weimar and Leipzig, 1989, *Die Abenteuer des braven Soldaten Schwejk*].

Ian Hay, *The First Hundred Thousand*, (Edinburgh, 1915; repr. Glasgow, 1985) [John Hay Beith].

Max Heinz, *Loretto. Aufzeichnungen eines Kriegsfreiwilligen*, (Berlin, 1929); tr. C. Ashleigh as *Loretto*, (New York, 1930).

Ernest Hemingway, *A Farewell to Arms*, (London, 1929; repr. 1977 etc.).

Ernst Johannsen, *Vier von der Infanterie. Ihre letzten Tage an der Westfront 1918*, (Berlin, 1929); tr. A. W. Wheen as *Four Infantrymen on the Western Front 1918*, (London, 1930).

David Jones, *In Parenthesis*, (London, 1937, repr. 1963).

Ernst Jünger, *In Stahlgewittern*, (Berlin, 1920; Stuttgart, 1981); tr. Basil Creighton as *The Storm of Steel*, (London, 1929, repr. 1942). [Realistic, but a more positive view of the war].

Ernst Jünger, *Das Wäldchen 125*, (Berlin, 1925); tr. Basil Creighton as *Copse 125*, (London, 1930).

Edlef Köppen, *Heeresbericht*, (Berlin, 1930); ed. Michael Gollbach (Kronberg, 1976, repr. Reinbek bei Hamburg, 1979); tr. as *Higher Command*, (London, 1931).

Andreas Latzko, *Friedensgericht*, (Zurich, 1918); tr. Ludwig Lewisohn as *Judgement of Peace*, (New York, 1919).

Andreas Latzko, *Menschen im Krieg*, (2. ed., Zurich 1918 [anonymous first ed., 1917]); tr. Adele Selyzer as *Men in Battle*, (London and New York, 1918).

Rose Macaulay, *Non-Combatants and Others*, (London, 1916, repr. 1986).

Frederic Manning, *Her Privates We*, (London, 1930), unexpurgated as *The Middle Parts of Fortune*, ed. Michael Howard, (London. 1977).

R. H. Mottram, *The Spanish Farm Trilogy*, (London, 1927 [1924-6]; Harmondsworth, 1979 etc.).

R. H. Mottram, *Ten Years Ago*, (London, 1928).

Theodor Pli(e)vier, *Des Kaisers Kulis*, (Berlin, 1929); ed. Hans-Harald Muller, (Cologne, 1981; repr. Munich, 1984 etc.); tr. Margaret Green as *The Kaiser's Coolies*, (New York, 1931) and by W. F. Clarke (London, 1932).

Ernest Raymond, *Tell England*, (London etc., 1922).

Ludwig Renn, *Krieg*, (Frankfurt/M., 1929); ed. H. Kipphardt and D. Pinkeneil, (Königsstein/T., 1979); tr. Willa and Edwin Muir as *War*, (New York and also London, 1929) [Arnold Vieth von Golssenau].

Ludwig Renn, *Nachkrieg*, (Vienna and Berlin, 1930); ed. H. Kipphardt and D. Pinkeneil, (Königsstein/T., 1979); tr. Willa and Edwin Muir as *After War*, (New York and also London, 1931).

Frank Richard, *Old Soldiers Never Die*, (London, 1933, repr. 1970).

Peter Riss, *Die große Zeit. Stahlbad Anno 17*, (Berlin, 1931).

Siegfried Sassoon, *Memoirs of an Infantry Officer*, (London, 1930, repr. 1965).

Meta Scheele, *Frauen im Krieg*, (Gotha, 1930).

Helen Zenna Smith, *"Not So Quiet...Stepdaughters of War"*, (London, 1930) [Evadne Price]. Repr. with an introduction by Barbara Hardy, (London, 1988).

Adrienne Thomas, *Die Katrin wird Soldat*, (Berlin, 1930; repr. Frankfurt/M., 1987; Munich, 1988); tr. Margaret Goldsmith as *Katrin Becomes a Soldier*, (Boston, 1931) and as *Cathérine Joins Up*, (London, 1931).

Georg von der Vring, *Soldat Suhren*, (Berlin, 1928); tr. Fred Hall as *Private Suhren*, (New York and London, 1928).

Josef Magnus Wehner, *Sieben vor Verdun. Ein Kriegsroman*, (Munich, [1930]). [An anti-Remarque militaristic novel].

Fritz von Unruh, *Opfergang*, (Berlin, 1919; Frankfurt/M., 1925), tr. C. A. Macartney as *The Way of Sacrifice*, (New York, 1928). [Original written in 1916, publication delayed by censor].

Rebecca West, *The Return of the Soldier*, (London, 1918, repr. 1988 etc.) [Cicely Isabel Fairfield].

Henry Williamson, *The Patriot's Progress*, (London, 1930).

Arnold Zweig, *Junge Frau von 1914*, (Berlin, 1931, Berlin and Weimar, 1970; Frankfurt/M., 1973 etc.) *Erziehung vor Verdun*, (1935, 1969, 1974 etc.) and *Der Streit um den Sergeanten Grischa*, (1928, 1969, 1972 etc.); tr. Eric Sutton as *Young Woman of 1914*, (London and also New York, 1932), *Education before Verdun*, (1936) and *The Case of Sergeant Grischa*, (1928). Three linked novels given here in sequence of action.

SOME FILMS

The Four Horsemen of the Apocalypse, (1921)

All Quiet on the Western Front, (1930)

Westfront 1918, (1930)

Tell England, (1930)

A Farewell to Arms, (1932)

Les croix de bois, (1932)

The Road Back, (1937)

La grande illusion, (1937)

All Quiet on the Western Front, (1979)